OONA

Books by Thomas Gallagher

Nonfiction
Fire at Sea: The Story of the Morro Castle
The Doctors' Story
The X-Craft Raid
Assault in Norway

Novels
The Gathering Darkness
The Monogamist
Oona O'

OONA O'

Thomas Gallagher

Harbrace Paperbound Library

HARCOURT BRACE JOVANOVICH
NEW YORK AND LONDON

The author wishes to express his deep gratitude to
HERMAN ZIEGNER
a warm friend and dedicated editor, who died without
warning as this book went to press.

Library of Congress Cataloging in Publication Data

Gallagher, Thomas Michael, date
Oona O'.

(Harbrace paperbound library ; HPL 67)
I. Title.
[PZ4.G162oo4]   [PS3557.A41157]   813'.5'4   75-33938
ISBN 0-15-671371-3

First Harbrace Paperbound Library edition 1976
A   B   C   D   E   F   G   H   I   J

O O N A O'

To John and Roz Gallagher

CHAPTER I

Via C Angelico 5
Villa Roseto
Fiesole, Firenze, Italy
April 23, 1953

Dear Jim & Nancy,

What I said last month when I called from Idlewild was true. I did not see or even write you before I left for fear I'd tell you too much. To Mama and Papa I can write pages and say nothing; to you two, my favorite brother and sister-in-law, I can't. Even in my letters to Mama and Papa, though, I'm going to have to start saying *something*. Everybody in the family reads them, and in a long postscript to the first reply I've received here, even Cathy, the "baby" of the family, asks what I'm doing in Europe and why I'm being so mysterious about it.

I still can't tell you the whole story, but for the present let me say this. For the past month I've been alone, living in Fiesole, in a villa with an Italian maid. The rent's paid for some time (so is the maid), but I myself have very little money. I had some, spent it, and am now living on the money

(4)

I received from having my return ticket refunded. Though I have been ill and have lost weight (where I can't afford to lose it), I'm well again and looking forward to receiving my clothes, linen, and books, which should arrive in a couple of days. The maid is simple, and my Italian less than fluent, so there's not much conversation. (Which reminds me. Could you send me some old magazines? If you don't subscribe to any, ask Mama and Papa for theirs. I'm dying to read, and even feel, a fat American magazine again.)

Anyway, to continue. I have some money in a bank in New York and can, I'm sure, if I become desperate, get a check cashed at the American Consulate. What really bothers me, though, is this: I took an apartment in New York under both my real name and an assumed name, to have some place to stay and leave my things. That doesn't make sense, does it? The two names, I mean. All right, the truth is that the apartment is under the name of a man (an eye surgeon, Dr. Anthony Friedensohn), and the furniture under mine. I bought the furniture and rugs and ordered drapes before leaving. The rent is paid up to May 15. There's a month's security as well, and I can manage to get another month's rent. But even if I *can* return to New York in June, which I doubt, I don't want the apartment and there's a two-year lease. The landlord should be willing (I keep telling myself) to void the lease. Vinyl and Formica and a new stove, new cabinet sink, and new refrigerator were installed in the kitchen; rubber tile was laid in the bathroom; the entire apartment was newly painted—and none of it at his expense.

What I'm coming to is this: If I can get the lease voided, would you two have the furniture, which is very expensive and has never been used, put in Lincoln Warehouse for me? Though they pack everything, even the dishes, themselves, an authorized person would have to be there with a list (which I would send you). I won't do anything until I hear from you, so please write soon.

Incidentally, don't think a maid here is luxurious. If you're not a maid yourself you can afford one.

Love
OONA O'

"That's it," Nancy said. "What do you think?"

"What can I think?" Jim O'Hagen said from a desk phone at the hospital. An intern at Bellevue, a tall, muscular man with big hands, captain of the Columbia football team before entering medical school, he had received a message to call his wife and for two hours (with Emergency jammed as a result of a three-car accident on Second Avenue) had wondered what could be wrong. Only once before had Nancy called the hospital, and then it had been to tell him his father had had a heart attack. Oona's letter was so ridiculously less important that for a moment he didn't know what to do with his relief, his excess energy. "You say she signed it 'Oona O' '? I swear, ever since grammar school she's been doing that. Signs all over the house. 'Property of Oona O'.' 'Oona O' at Work.' 'Oona O' Asleep.' She even had arrows pointing to 'Oona O's Room.' "

"Forget the signature, will you?" She could hear his exasperated breathing through the receiver, could almost see his face harden with anger, his white jacket wrinkle and pull under the hidden influence of his strength. Oona and her problems again. Oona killed him with her problems. "I know you're busy, Jim. But you won't be home tomorrow either and I thought I'd get a letter off tonight. She sounds as if . . ."

"She always sounds 'as if.' That's the trouble. Who's this eye surgeon she's talking about, this Dr. Friedensohn? Do you know? Because I don't. The apartment's under his name, she says, and the furniture's under hers. Did you ever hear of anything more like Oona than that? Suppose he's still living there. How are we going to have the lease voided? Is the guy dead? Has he given up the apartment? Is he living in Italy with her, or what? I mean why does everything concerning Oona have to be involved? Why must it always be impossible to connect what she wants you to do with how, or why, she wants you to do it?"

Silence. No argument from Nancy, who had known Oona longer than she had him, and who knew her now, who saw her now, in a much more intimate and like-minded way than he did. Oona had introduced him to Nancy and been Nancy's maid of honor at their wedding. Oona and Nancy had gone to college together, they had lived in the Village together, gone out with men together, discussed sex and marriage and all the rest of it together. So no argument from Nancy, who wanted to be—was—loyal to both of them.

"All right," he went on, "tell her we'll take care of the furniture for her. Only ask her what it's all about, will you? Tell her to stop being so mysterious all the time. . . . I have to go, Nancy. If I don't see you tomorrow night, I'll be there first thing Sunday morning. Bye."

"Wait a minute, will you? If you're not coming home tomorrow night, I'd like to see a movie or something. Do you mind—Doctor?"

He smiled. Just that morning he had opened his eyes and found himself inches away from, and looking up at, her right breast lying in the cradle of her chest, its summit crossed with sleep wrinkles. He had buried his face there, and the warm irrepressible honey of her, the smell of a woman who enjoyed being one with a man, whose natural instincts gave her joy rather than feelings of inferiority, had passed over him with something of the effect of music on his relaxed and rested nerves. Then the alarm had gone off and there were showers to be taken, oranges to be squeezed, coffee to be made.

"See the movie, darling. I'm sorry. Even if I do get home, it won't be until after midnight."

"See you then, Jim. Bye."

"Bye."

CHAPTER II

Oona O'Hagen's eye surgeon, Tony Friedensohn, was neither dead, nor living with her in Italy, nor occupying the apartment from which she wanted her furniture removed. Nor could Oona, as Jim and Nancy suggested in their letter to her, fly home without delay, before her lease on the villa ran out and she found herself penniless in a foreign country.

As was often the case when Oona said, "I still can't tell you the whole story," what she had meant was that the story was far from over and that even she did not know how it was going to end. Had she known, she would have been no less diffuse in what she told Jim and Nancy, for with Oona the extraneous matter was always the gold, that which made an experience what it really was.

She had met Tony Friedensohn the year before in New York, at one of those cocktail parties where no one knows, or makes any real effort to get to know, anyone else. Oona had a way at a party, though, especially an awkward one, of looking at a stranger as if there were no one in the world she so much wanted to meet. Who are you at the other end of this restraint? she seemed to say with those wildly beautiful green eyes of hers that belonged as much in a tree as in a living room. Not that she ever neglected a friend at a party—on the contrary, but a stranger, if only by being unknown, was more susceptible to the hope and wonder she felt, or wanted to feel, toward all human relationships.

So when Tony Friedensohn noticed her noticing him and went over and offered to get her a drink, the very warmth of her response ("I'd *love* a martini. I really would.") made him hesitate a moment before getting it. Either she was extraordinarily appreciative of small favors, or an alcoholic with some kind of superstition against getting a drink herself. Still, there was something wonderful and exciting about being made this responsible for a beautiful girl's happiness.

"Olive, onion, or twist of lemon?" he went on. "They seem to have everything."

"Mist of lemon, then, all right? The twist and that's all. Don't drop the peel in after you twist it. If you do"—she pressed his arm—"if you let it marinate, even for a minute, I'll never forgive you."

All she was doing was having a little fun—reacting to a dull party by saying, in effect, Thank goodness someone here is human. But she could fill her voice (and face) with such feeling that the words themselves often fell off center, in some other path of meaning. This isn't where inane chatter belongs, a listener could not help thinking, not unless I'm crazy—am I crazy?

"I'll be back in a minute," he said, and turned toward a sideboard laden with bottles and buckets of ice at the other end of the room.

Watching him go, and even more struck from behind by his tallness and elongated El Greco neck, Oona wondered who he was, what he did, why he had come over to her and all. She could see from the way he passed through or around the unwieldy clusters of people that he had developed a slightly forward-reaching spine in deference to short people (the shorter the people in his way, the farther forward he reached in begging their pardon), and she decided to like that about him at least for the time being, until it proved to be a conceit or something. But who was he? She went through the possibilities in her mind and decided that he could be almost anyone nice. She rejected mean thoughts about him, but that was about all.

There was a much-used liquor ad in the magazines at the time, and though Tony Friedensohn could have been, and was in fact often mistaken for, the man in the ad, though Oona had seen the ad herself a hundred times, she did not associate him with it. Tony Friedensohn had the same tall tennis player's figure and the same sharp features set in a face so lean that the cheekbones, as Oona later put it, looked like "shiny buttons," but he also had (and this was perhaps why she didn't make the association) the same ability to be taken for a lawyer, an account executive, a customer's man, a management consultant, or even for what he actually was, a doctor.

It might not have been significant, but as Oona was to find out later, this unconscious adaptability on Tony Friedensohn's part, his ability to harmonize with whatever decently reasonable estimate was made of him, carried even to his clothes, or rather, to the way he could fit into a ready-made size 36 long without a single alteration other than trouser cuffs. In fact, when he first returned with her drink, she did not find him interesting at all except for one thing, his smile, which made everything else about him at least potentially interesting in that it didn't suggest pleasure so much as uncertainty as to what to *do* with pleasure. Give me a hand with this, will you? he seemed to say. I'm not used to it. He blinked, his eyes moistened, and his mouth, well, for several seconds it was impossible to tell whether he was just getting over being sad or tentatively on his way to being happy. And the thing was, Oona became so involved in the struggle, she was so glad when the edges of sadness disappeared and the smile became a smile she could really count on, that she felt like cheering.

One afternoon after they had known each other

only a few weeks, they drove to a restaurant on Long Island and sat (it was three o'clock and the place was empty) in the garden over a light lunch. The breeze smelled of new grass and salt, and they could see, far out on the Sound, swatches of sail blinking with sunlight like prizewinning parts of the water itself.

"Well, let's forget it," Oona said, though no one had spoken. She had been trying to think of something exceptionally nice to say to him, and that was what came out.

"What do you mean?" he said.

"If you're not going to say nice things to me, let's forget it," she said, switching the whole thing around. Then because his smile began jamming up on him, she felt guilty. "No, I'm kidding. I don't know why I said that. Don't pay any attention to me."

"I say things to myself," he said. "Then think they've been said already. Or they're not worth saying."

"Let me be the judge of that, will you?" She had crossed her legs and was swinging her foot back and forth with her shoe dangling from her toes. She'd been doing it unconsciously, but now, in the silence that followed her remark, something momentous seemed involved in whether or not the shoe fell. They looked down at it together in silence, sharing its fate as they might have their own. It was a splendid moment for both of them, and after a while Tony's face reddened and he said, "You want to be the judge?"

After that they met every day, sometimes even twice a day. Oona would wait for him in the lobby of the Institute of Ophthalmology on 165th Street, or at a coffee shop on Broadway just up from the Institute, or he'd drive downtown, if she had to work late, and meet her. She knew that he had spent years in Italy, that he had an eye clinic in Florence and that he was in New York only for a year's special study at the Institute. What she didn't know, and what he didn't tell her until it was too late, was that he had an Italian wife in Florence. His wife had remained behind, he said, to manage property she owned there.

Whatever a girl should or might want to do when a man tells her a thing like that, she hardly ever falls out of love. She doesn't even want to if, like Oona, she's pregnant and the man says he intends to do something about it and then actually does do something. Tony wrote and told his wife what had happened, and it was not until after she had agreed, after a long exchange of letters, to a divorce, and not until after Tony had decided to leave Florence permanently and practice in New York, that he and Oona decided on an apartment.

The wife, however, had imposed one condition: that Tony return to Florence and see her before they separated permanently. Tony had to return to Florence anyway, to settle matters pertaining to his practice there, so after discussing the matter with Oona, he had agreed.

Oona, by now six months pregnant, did not want to have her baby in New York where her mother and father would naturally want to meet the father (and perhaps even demand to see a marriage license), so she and Tony decided to go to Europe together. They would rent, under Oona's name, the smallest, least expensive villa in Fiesole (a suburb of Florence and only four miles away) so that Tony could make a clean break in Florence and, at the same time, be with Oona when she had the baby. They would then use the villa as a base for motoring around Europe before returning to their apartment in New York.

But nothing worked out as planned, and once in Europe, Oona discovered other things that in New York she wasn't told. She knew that Tony was born in America and that he'd met his wife in Florence during the summer of 1946 after he'd graduated from Princeton. What she didn't know was that it was his wife (and not his late parents) who had financed his medical education in Florence, and that before their marriage he had become, at her request, an Italian citizen. Though older and much stronger than Tony, Mrs. Friedensohn was still beautiful, with one of those Etruscan faces that never sag or take on fat. More than that—much more, apparently, in view of what happened—she was extremely wealthy.

One day about a month after Tony and Oona had been living together at the villa, he had breakfast with her as usual, kissed her goodbye as usual, and drove down to Florence on business as usual. Oona knew he had many things to settle before leaving Italy for good, and because his separation from his wife was one of them, she did not press him for details. She had not met and did not want to meet—or even talk about—his wife. Instead she concentrated in all their conversations on their plans, their marriage, their future together.

On this day, however, Tony returned from Florence much earlier than usual, in the middle of the afternoon, and his wife was with him. Oona heard their footsteps and saw them—through a window facing on the driveway where they'd parked their car—before they saw her. This alone had a very powerful effect on Oona, who had almost a child's capacity to let what happened to her, in her mind and emotions, happen whether it had a "right" to happen or not. Indeed, many more things happened to her as a result of this habit of mind than would have if she had, so to speak, laid down the law.

The sun was hot and glary all around Tony and his wife as they approached the house, and what made Oona think of her swollen belly, what made her, that is, conscious of a feeling that it was two against two (Tony and his wife against the baby and her) was that she was watching them unseen from a dark, shady place. She remembered her childhood summers at the seashore in Jersey, how she and her brother Jim would crawl under the lifeguard's upside-down boat on the beach to get out of the sun and how just being under it, in the shade, with the cool sand against their skin, made them different from "sun people." Watching Tony and his wife from her shady place at the window was like that. They became "sun people" and she that same tomboy under the lifeguard's boat with Jim. She saw them with something like a child's awe and wonder, and with her whole being she knew that she was as different from them as she had been from the owners of all those arms and legs around the lifeguard's boat at the beach in Jersey.

If the woman was Tony's wife (and Oona knew she could be no one else), their coming together to see her could only mean that his wife had reached an understanding with him that overrode her own understanding with him. Otherwise Tony would have told her his wife was coming. The villa had no phone, but he would have called the telegraph office in Fiesole (as he had done before) and had a message sent. What bothered her was not her appearance so much (though she didn't enjoy the prospect of being seen pregnant by Mrs. Friedensohn) as Tony's allowing her to be unprepared to meet his wife. In New York he had allowed her to believe he was unmarried; now he was allowing her to be unprepared to meet his wife.

There was a knock, and when the maid opened the door, and Oona saw that their eyes were not used to the darkness of the villa, she said, "Be careful. The last step is missing."

She said it to be mean (there were no steps at all), but if she could be pregnant in front of them like this, Mrs. Friedensohn could grope around for steps that didn't exist. It didn't work, though. Either Tony had warned his wife about her, or Mrs. Friedensohn was familiar with the villa.

After Oona had given the maid, who adored Tony and thought he was Oona's husband, the afternoon off, Tony, with all the color gone from his lips, and his wife, her cameo beauty still intact but obviously too old to have a baby herself, came forward to greet Oona. Even if Tony hadn't been Jewish, Oona would have been struck by the sheer size of the crucifix hanging round his wife's neck. Solid gold and weighing, Oona thought, at least as much as her traveling clock, it reached almost to the waist and made Mrs. Friedensohn something like a female pope.

"Oona, I don't deny I'm the father of your child," Tony said. "I never will deny it. I'll give the child my name. I'll support it . . . but I cannot marry you."

They were standing face to face, chaperoned from a distance by Mrs. Friedensohn, in the same room where two days before they had decided to return to New York as soon after the birth as they could travel. For a moment they remained as they were, Oona with her eyes on a lovely birthmark on his cheek, as though the very last of his qualities were concentrated there, and he with his mouth all distorted as a result of the effort he was making to be firm, reasonable, grieved, and sincere. When it became obvious even to him that he was none of these things, he turned to his wife, and it was at this moment, as their eyes met, that Oona suddenly recognized Tony. She could see his face, really *see* it, because it no longer represented qualities that could not be seen. And that smile of his, that hesitant alternative to sadness: she suddenly realized that in New York it had been the truest thing about him and that it was still the truest thing about him. He was a deeply sad man, a man preoccupied with whatever vague something in the past had made him a coward. Like a hidden deformity it haunted him, made even his smile sad.

Mrs. Friedensohn, one of those women who are both fortified and calmed by the tension of others, came forward and stood slightly in front of Tony facing Oona. In perfect English she said that Oona could have the baby at their expense in Florence. A private hospital room had already been reserved for the purpose so that Oona could move in whenever she felt the birth was near. Afterward, when Oona was well enough to leave, she (Mrs. Friedensohn) would become the baby's legal mother and make a settlement whereby Oona could do as she pleased for a year.

Oona would always associate this very formal speech of Mrs. Friedensohn's with feet, because all during it Tony, standing just behind his wife, kept stamping his in slow motion. Only there was no sound; the stamp always stopped in time and became a kind of press. This indeed was the extraneous kind of thing that made an experience what it really was for Oona—the "gold" that often saved her. She had made no conscious effort to notice Tony's feet or to avoid what Mrs. Friedensohn was saying to her. She just couldn't help becoming involved in nonessentials, what she herself called "cutting-room stuff"—the slip-ups and gaucheries that art, so called, excluded.

What really saved her, though, was his wife's feet, which she probably would not have noticed if it hadn't been for Tony's stamping his. They were doll's feet, very small, but so thick and stubby that they didn't go with the rest of her at all. The insteps were so high that the laces of her shoes, let alone the tongues, could barely contain them.

"Is your dress Italian or French?" Oona said, partly to diversify the conversation and partly to avoid thanking her for having ugly feet. If she had had beautiful feet too, Oona would not have known what to do. She might have accepted Mrs. Friedensohn's offer.

"Italian," Mrs. Friedensohn said.

"It's lovely," Oona said, and that was all. Mrs. Friedensohn glanced at Tony, nodded to Oona, and prepared to leave.

At first Oona thought they had decided to wait until she was forced to come to them for help. But watching them, watching Mrs. Friedensohn especially, she changed her mind. They were leaving because Mrs. Friedensohn knew she knew. Of course. That was why, at the mere mention of the word "lovely," her face had hardened so. Her feet did go with the rest of her, with her marriage to Tony, her power over him, her wealth, her wanting the child before it was even born—the whole key to her character was in those feet of hers. And the giveaway was the lovely dress, when she said "lovely" instead of "ugly." Of course. How obvious! She glanced at Tony and decided that there was even a chance that he had stamped his feet so she would notice his wife's feet. Unconsciously he might have been saying something like, I can't marry you, Oona but take a look at the feet on the one I *am* married to. It might have been his way of saying he was sorry. It just might have been.

She stood gripping the edge of her sandals with her toes, wishing they would leave and trying desperately to control herself until they did. If they had simply walked to the door and closed it behind them, she would have controlled herself. But Mrs. Friedensohn went over for her bag and parasol with such unhurried ease, and yet with her spine so straight and so much like a fork in her head, that Oona couldn't help herself. Regrettably, for it made her so moral, so desperate, so American, she said, "Do you know your boy deceived me, Mrs. Friedensohn? Do you know this never would have happened if he had simply *told* me he was married?"

Mrs. Friedensohn waited until she had reached the door. Then, without moving a single vertebra in that precious spine of hers, she turned around. "You should manage your affairs more intelligently, Miss O'Hagen," she said, and walked out.

Oona stood there like someone born on Amsterdam Avenue (where she *was* born), because it was true, she hadn't managed her affairs intelligently. She had trusted Tony first and discovered the reasons for not trusting him second, and now Tony and his wife "looked good" and she didn't. And in court, if she brought them to court, they would look even better. Her instincts might be finer than theirs, she might be a much finer person all around, but that didn't matter because she had not managed her affairs intelligently.

A minute or two passed, then Tony came back alone, with his medical bag, and said he had left his wife in the car on the pretext of taking Oona's blood pressure.

"Listen to me, Oona," he said. "My wife refused to give me a divorce weeks ago, when we first arrived. I put off telling you about it, thinking I could reason with her. I can't. She's determined to remain my wife, and lawyers here tell me there's nothing I can do. If I were an American citizen I could go back with you, I *would* go back with you, and get a divorce. But I'm an Italian citizen and divorce is not possible in Italy. Even if I were to go back with you anyway, it would do no good. My wife has money and influence over here. My passport would be invalidated. I'd be forced to return to Italy. You'd be even worse off than you are now."

Whenever Oona had time to think, as she did this time, she felt too many different ways to act only one way, so she didn't act any way. She was going to call him a "wop" for becoming an Italian citizen, but she didn't because by the time he'd finished speaking she had already begun to remember nice things about him, like the time he took her on a tour of the Institute of Ophthalmology in New York. Actually, he was making his afternoon rounds that day, and when Oona asked if she could go along, he gave her a pad and pencil and told her to pretend she was making notes. The clinic was crowded when they walked in, and what struck Oona immediately was how so many of the patients seemed to know and love Tony. One little boy in particular stood out because Tony had operated on him himself. The boy had come in three weeks before with malignant tumors in both eyes (retinoblastoma, Tony called it), and though Tony had had to remove the left eye (there was a patch over it) and the boy knew he'd removed it, the boy seemed to become much less fidgety and nervous when Tony, after introducing Oona to the parents, began touching the boy, just touching him, with his hands. Oona noticed that particularly and she remembered a remark someone had made in the doctors' cafeteria one day, about Friedensohn's having "good hands."

Tony, meanwhile, had taken his stethoscope and blood-pressure strap from his bag and was asking Oona to roll up the sleeve of her robe.

"I thought you said it was a pretext."

"It was. But I'm here, so I might as well see what it is. And if you don't mind, Oona, I'd like a urine specimen to take with me."

"Never mind," Oona said. "I'm perfectly all right."

"You've been having headaches and dizzy spells, you said. Your ankles are swollen. Please let me take your blood pressure, Oona."

"I said I'm all right. Now leave, will you?"

"I'll send a doctor up from Florence, then."

"I'll get my own doctor. Don't you send one. If you do, I'll refuse to see him. Now will you please leave?" She was going to cry if he stayed any longer; she had to get rid of him. "Mama's waiting for you. Go on!"

After he had closed the door behind him, she turned her head sharply to the side and down, chin in the crook of her shoulder, to cry. She wanted to cry, tears would have been comforting, but too much had happened too fast—her whole position in Italy had become, in fifteen minutes, too untenable and absurd—for comfort to matter. Outwitted and deceived by that woman and betrayed by Tony, she had crossed the ocean not to get married but to have an illegitimate child in a country where she had no friends, no money, no doctor and no hospital rights except on Mrs. Friedensohn's terms. Yet an outsider seeing her at that moment would have said she looked more contemplative than frightened, and she *was* more contemplative, for at the heart of her predicament, defining it on the one hand and confirming Mrs. Friedensohn's admonition on the other ("You should handle your affairs more intelligently, Miss O'Hagen"), was the realization that not once since she'd become pregnant had she given any serious consideration to the possibility of her child's being illegitimate. Not once had she entertained doubts about Tony's loyalty or given any thought to how she might protect herself, on her terms, if he turned out to be disloyal. Was she naïve, simple-minded, unconsciously self-destructive, an Irish ignoramous with misplaced courage, or what, to be this unacquainted with how things really were in this world? Twenty-four years old and she was only beginning to realize what an encumbrance innocence was, what a weapon trust was, for the person trusted, what a stink went with safety, what cowardice was needed to win, and even how close love was to rottenness.

She could go to the American Consulate and expose both of them; she knew that, but unless she actually gave birth *at* the Consulate, on American soil, so to speak, it would do no good to expose them. Tony wouldn't deny he was the father, and he was an Italian, not an American, citizen. The case would be brought to an Italian court, where Tony would be awarded at least partial rights to a child he both acknowledged and was willing to support. He would be willing to forgo all such rights (weak men were often very fair), but his wife, who thought the child was half hers because Tony had fathered it, would not be. Oona wanted the baby to be with *her* when she left the country, wanted it to be an American citizen, and, most important of all, wanted that woman to have no say in its upbringing.

If she could intimidate Tony, a grown man, what
ghastly thing would she do to a child?

Jim and Nancy O'Hagen, in New York, were told
most of the above details in a long letter from Oona
dated May 4, 1953, a letter in which she went on to
say:

Anyway, that should explain why I cannot fly
home for the present. I expect to have the baby in a
few weeks, maybe sooner. But I'm not worried
about that so much as I am about not being able to
go to a hospital. Even if I could afford to go, I
wouldn't for fear of red tape. Italy is as bureaucratic
as they say Russia is, and I will not have the baby
shuttled like something unnotarized from one office
to another—let alone taken from me. So it will be
quite primitive here in the villa, with probably a
midwife and my maid.

Another reason I cannot fly home is that I
haven't the fare. Yesterday the milk bill arrived
(and I *live* on milk); today the shipping bill for my
trunk (which has just been unloaded at Genoa).
Pretty soon, though I'm living in the kind of villa
you read about in travel folders, I'll be rolling my
own cigarettes. I'll get home somehow, though,
later this year. Right now, I want to get the apart-

ment and furniture off my mind. I'm enclosing a
personal check, made out to you, for Lincoln Warehouse, for the packing, moving, and one or two
months' storage. When they bill you (I have exactly
$280 in my New York bank), please fill in the
amount and sign it over to them.

Also, I'm enclosing two keys, one for the downstairs door to 84 Irving Place (a block up from
Pete's Bar, Nancy, where we used to go after classes
at the New School), and the other for the door to
the apartment itself (4-C). My name is supposedly
Friedensohn and that's what you'll see on the door:
Dr. & Mrs. Anthony Friedensohn. (Funny, but now
that I've given you the address, I'm more there, at
84 Irving Place, than I am here. I can see you
walking in, your faces as you switch on the light, the
glances you exchange. Because I *was* prepared to
love that apartment, just as you two love yours. The
drapes aren't up or anything, but maybe, when you
first walk in, you'll be able to see how I might have
loved it.)

As for the items themselves, I'm enclosing a list.
The small radio, steam iron, and linen were supposed to be sent with my clothes. If they weren't
(and I won't know whether they were or not until
my trunk arrives from Genoa), please include them
and anything else I may have forgotten to list, with
what you send to Lincoln. If Jim thinks he can sell
the Venetian blinds and radiator covers to some

dealer in the Village (together they came to over
$200)—okay. If he thinks I should keep them on
the chance that I may be able to use them later
(though right now the money is more essential)—
okay.

One other thing. If it isn't too much trouble,
would you go to the apartment at night? I have
reasons. And please walk up. If you don't, McManus
will ask a million questions. He's the super and on
the elevator. Meanwhile, to give you time to go up
and look around and make arrangements, I'll wait
two or three days before writing the landlord.
Tony—now that his wife has cowed him—wants the
lease voided as much as I want the furniture put in
Lincoln, so in my letter to the landlord I'll say, with
an accompanying letter from Tony, which I already
have, that illness prevents my return to America at
this time, that I've authorized my brother, James
O'Hagen, to put my furniture in storage for me, and
that I will, if the apartment cannot be rented by
June 15, pay another month's rent.

Incidentally, if there's a large unopened box from
Macy's in the living room, will you let me know?
They're lamps that are to be picked up and credited
to my account. A smaller box will be more dishes or
glasses, and they're to be picked up too. I told
McManus that he could have the two or three odd
chairs in the living room (not the six new black ones
from Chivari), and any cleaning stuff in the two

closets in the hall. But the sponge mop and ironing board (in the bedroom closet) I'd like sent to Lincoln. And if there are any papers in the night-table drawer, would you send them to me? They should be receipts.

I absolutely hate having to involve you in my tangled affairs, and I wouldn't if there were anyone else I could trust without hurting. This same letter addressed to Mama and Papa would break their hearts. They're still so Irish Catholic, and I don't want to worry them, or rather, test them. They're not small-minded, I don't mean that—far from it. What I mean is, well, take the Italians here. Religion to them is like the crust on their wonderful bread. They break through it with their teeth or fingers, dip the softer part in garlic oil, and then eat everything, crust and all. They don't discard the crust, or eat *only* the crust, because that would be a waste of the loaf itself. Do you understand me at all? I'm not associating Mama and Papa with zwieback, dumplings, or anything else. But you know yourself, they're about as Italian as Haile Selassie.

Oh, by the way, I'm enclosing a telephone-bill adjustment for forty-eight cents. I hate to make out a check for that amount (I have only a few and I need them), so would you please pay it for me? If McManus questions you at all when the stuff is being removed (he likes me and is very nice), tell him you're my brother and show him the enclosed authorization. Actually, it's none of his business (the furniture is definitely mine and in my name), but I feel responsible for the apartment, and in a way I am.

Please write soon. I'm anxious.

Love,

OONA O'

P.S. The authorization, notarized at the American Express office in Florence, and the furniture list, are enclosed.

May 4, 1953

TO WHOM IT MAY CONCERN

I, Oona O'Hagen (Mrs. A. Friedensohn), in full possession of my faculties and of my own free will, do hereby authorize my brother, James O'Hagen, to remove and place in storage any furniture and effects belonging to me at 84 Irving Place—Apt. 4-C—New York City. He may use his discretion and take whatever steps he may find necessary to execute these matters.

OONA O'HAGEN

(*Mrs. A. Friedensohn*)

FURNITURE TO BE STORED

BEDROOM

Bed (*mattress & spring, headboard and foot-board*)
Dresser & Mirror
Rocking Chair
Night Table
Bookcase

LIVING ROOM

2 Soft Chairs
Small French Sofa
6 Black Italian Chairs
1 Black Table (brown linen tablecloth)
Radio-Phonograph (records inside cabinet)
Indian Writing Desk
Teakwood Chest
Bombe Commode

KITCHEN

Stemware
Bar Stool
Dishes & Glasses
Silverware (in table drawer under stove & closet drawers)
Pots & Utensils
Bread Box

Garbage Pail
Electric Rotisserie

BATHROOM

Hamper
Wastebasket
Shower & Window Curtains
White Rug & Toilet-Seat Cover
Cabinet

MISCELLANEOUS

Large Wooden Salad Bowl
Black Iron Candlesticks (on bookcase)
Venetian Blinds (in both rooms)
3 Radiator Covers (black, white and brown)
15 Framed Pictures (contents of dresser drawers)
Ashtrays of various shapes and sizes (about 10)
3 Small Oval Gray Rugs (on top shelf, closet in
   hall)
2 Portable Closets in Hallway
3 Clocks (one electric)
1 Ironing Board (bedroom closet) and any other
   odds & ends forgotten.

CHAPTER III

Irving Place was quiet and small-townish in the twilight, an odd, shopless bit of street only a few parked cars away from the political and religious spasms of Union Square, the fierce commercial hysteria of Klein's, the fume-filled ferociousness of Fourteenth Street running from river to river like a huge moving belt jammed with buses, trucks, traffic cops, nationalities, and the feverish immigrant desire to "get ahead."

At Nineteenth Street a Bowery bum, his face as familiar around the streets of New York as a building excavation, scuffed up to Jim and Nancy for a handout.

"Mister, no horseshit, I mean it," he said, but seeing Nancy (apparently for the first time), he stepped back and bowed in apology. He probably only meant to nod in apology, but it turned out to be quite a bow by the time he got through with it. "I'm sorry, miss. I didn't mean—I didn't see—"

As a boy Jim O'Hagen had been deeply troubled by the bums who occupied a certain park bench in his neighborhood. (If bums had children, didn't that mean *his* father could become one?) Even as

an intern at Bellevue he had had to get used to what
the staff called the "Bowery trade," the bums who
came in every night with cuts, bruises, concussions,
broken bones and hemorrhages, who fell down
cellar stairs, suffered frostbitten toes and ears and
the senseless onslaughts of muggers and brutal
teen-agers—who were even hit by cars and left at the
curb while the drivers ostensibly drove off for help.
After a while, though, their intimate knowledge of
degradation and loss, their quiet acceptance of pain
(sometimes the pain he himself had to inflict to
treat them) and the way they seemed to epitomize
the inexplicable unfairness of life—whatever it was
that made them both more and less human than
anybody else—had a strangely humbling effect on
him.

"Believe me, miss." The bum was advancing
upon them again. "I'm sorry."

He came close enough for them to smell the inner
rot and putrefaction oozing through his clothes,
close enough for them to see his bloodless skin and
the vague, unfocused expression in which he had
secluded himself. And yet there was a wistful gen-
tlemanliness in the way he accepted Jim's quarter,
the grace that comes to the man who knows he's
through, wants to be forgotten, and then goes on
living as if only the memory of civilization still
existed.

What did such a man *do?* Jim had heard the

student nurses ask that question and had asked it himself—had gone himself on walks around the Bowery in an effort to find out. And the answer was simply that such a man sat in doorways, lingered in woody warmth over a mug of beer, and took wintry delights in fifty-cent flops. He never sought trouble, never maliciously harmed anyone, and was never mindful of the cigarette, drink or plate of soup beyond the one he was presently enjoying. Living always close to death in misty consciousness of potter's field, he accepted each day with an un-protesting completeness that was beyond the ca-pacity of the hardworking and respectable.

Something like dignity, the serenity of the damned, seemed to slide along with the man, a gargoyle with eyes of stone, as he continued on down toward the Bowery's "21," the Fourteenth Street White Rose Bar. A plate of thick soup and a beer, maybe a shot with a beer chaser, and he'd sit there, just sit there and dream, until told in a friendly but firm way to "get moving."

Jim and Nancy walked along in silence for a while. Then as they approached 84 Irving Place, Jim said, "We unlock the downstairs door and walk in as if someone upstairs gave us a buzz."

"But wouldn't McManus, if he's in the hallway, hear the buzz?"

"Not if it's a long hallway, or one of those L-shaped affairs, or he's getting on or off the elevator. But if he does say anything, we'll just show him Oona's authorization, that's all. We're going to have to speak to him anyway—before we get Lincoln over here."

Before he had finished speaking, a man and woman turned the corner from Gramercy Park, entered the building, unlocked the front door, and walked in.

"Perfect," Jim said. "McManus'll be taking them up to their apartment. Come on."

They entered a hallway so thickly carpeted that it was hard to believe any of the tenants had, or were allowed to have, children. The building had apparently been renovated from basement to roof except for the elevator, which was of very early vintage, with a grated cage around its shaft and manually operated sliding gates at each floor. They could see the cables moving and hear the chain sliding along the concrete in the basement.

"No sense hurrying," Jim said as they started up the stairs. "Elevator has to start down before we can go all the way up."

When they reached the second floor, the elevator stopped and so did they, Jim using the time to light a cigarette. Why, though, did everything connected with Oona have to be complicated? Why couldn't they have come in the daytime? Why did she have to have "reasons" for their coming at night? For that matter, why couldn't they have gone directly to

McManus, explained the situation, shown him the authorization, and proceeded like non-criminals to the apartment? Even as a child, at home, if she knew something you wanted to know—something simple like What play are Ma and Pa seeing to-night?—she'd start "from the beginning" and be as patient with you as what she said would be ir-relevant. There had to be asides, qualifications, and even other possible interpretations with Oona, who couldn't tie her shoelaces without knotting them.

"Never again," he whispered as they waited. "If we have to sneak around like this, she can get someone else to help her."

"She has a reason, Jim. She must have. And besides, we have the authorization."

"Exactly! We have the authorization."

"Listen, did you ever go to a movie with her? If you think this is bad, don't ever go to a movie with her."

"What a comparison! Did I ever go to a *movie* with her. Anything worse than this makes this that much better—is that it?"

As the elevator started down, they started up again. No one saw them on the third floor, nor on the fourth, where they tiptoed around, Jim with the key ready in his hand, to 4-C, a black metal door whose nameplate (DR. & MRS. ANTHONY FRIEDENSOHN) made an ironic epitaph for what was buried there.

Switching on lights wherever possible, they walked into an apartment neither large nor small, vacant nor lived-in—an apartment no one else in the family knew about and one that gave out very little information anyway. There were sheets covering soft chairs on whose seats lampshades or odd pillows had been put, excelsior wrappings around the legs of a French provincial Magnavox, and cardboard protectors around the rosewood corners of a tambour desk. Italian chairs still to be sat on, and yet so characteristically tagged "Rush Order" at what had undoubtedly been Oona's insistence, stood here and there between a bureau and an unhung mirror, a lampstand and an Indian teak-wood chest, an electric rotisserie and a bathroom cabinet with a three-way mirror.

"Here are the receipts she was talking about," Nancy said. "And that unopened box from Ma-cy's."

"Do you think they lived here?" Jim said. "I mean it all still looks so crazy."

He went through an archway to the kitchen. He wanted to see the whole apartment—kitchen, bath-room, bedroom—right away, and then go back over everything carefully the second time. That's why Nancy had found the receipts and the unopened box from Macy's and he hadn't. She was willing to let the rest of the apartment wait. It wasn't going to run away, and meanwhile there was all this, the whole living room, to take in.

She looked around. Jim was right, though, about the craziness. Oona had a flair for clothes rather than for furnishings, which to her were things of various shapes and sizes that did not fit around your body, legs or head, and so could not be related to you or even assimilated by you in a room or apartment. Oona knew what constituted a beautiful piece of furniture, and knew also when she was in a room full of beautiful pieces graciously arranged. What she didn't know was how the effect was accomplished, and especially how a person expressed herself, or himself, by putting this piece here, and that piece there, and the other piece (which Oona would definitely have put in the middle) in the room as you entered.

"About the size of ours," Jim said, coming back. "Small but adequate."

"Oh, look at this," Nancy said.

It was Oona's First Holy Communion prayer book, a glossy white, rotund little thing with a navel-like hollow in the middle of the cover, and set in the hollow, behind a tiny celluloid window, a gold image of Christ on the Cross.

She handed it to Jim, who looked at it as he had once looked at his own. Everybody had leftover pieties, even Oona, who would be the first to deny it. He recalled the day he had found her alone and crying (she must have been ten or eleven) on the

roof of their apartment house. She wouldn't tell
him what was wrong and he had never found out,
but the sorrowfulness of the moment, the way it
seemed to make him really her brother for the first
time, had always stayed with him. Had she made
her confirmation that day? Funny how none of the
facts, just the feeling of love mixed with the black
heat of the sun and the smell of tar, had remained
with him.

"You should see yourself," Nancy said.

"What do you mean?" He put the prayer book
aside.

"You and Oona, that's all. Both of you. Two of a
kind."

"We don't believe any more, you mean?"

"Just the opposite. You *do* believe."

"Nancy, stop sounding like every other Catholic,
will you?"

Yet as they continued to browse about the apartment, trying a chair here, sliding open a drawer
there, and touching smaller things like stemware,
clocks, and Greenwich Village trays and vases,
things toward whose size and shape they began to
feel a kindly interest, their silence became so iden-
tified in Jim's mind with Oona's absence that he
went back to the prayer book. His sister was dead.
She had died in childbirth in Italy, and he and
Nancy were there doing what people do when
someone dies. He had urged Oona in a letter to go

to a hospital in Florence at Friedensohn's expense,
but the death thought came less from his failure
thus far to receive a reply than from the unlived-
in apartment itself, the assembled but unused furniture, and the sense both gave of a life intercepted.

He got out a short note from Oona dated May 10,
1953:

Dear Jim & Nancy,

No hurry, but how do you think Mama and Papa
are going to react to my having a baby? I could say
that I had the marriage annulled, or that I'd adopted
a baby here whose mother died in childbirth, whichever you think they'd be more likely to accept. If
neither, should I leave the baby here until I can get
settled in New York? The future has become so
immediate, and so full of questions. If anything
should happen to me, Mama and Papa can have
everything except the dining room table and chairs.
You two can have those.

Love,
Oona O'

"You think anything's happened to her?" he
said.

"That occurred to me too."

"Maybe I got it from you."

"Anyway, nothing's happened to her. I'm sure of it." She held up a large wooden salad bowl. "You see this? And look at the candlestick holders. Look at the stemware."

"Ours exactly. I know—*cat*."

" 'Cat' my eye. I love her for buying them. Only it's crazy the way she can go through the racks at Altman's and Lord and Taylor's and have so much confidence about clothes and all and then have no confidence when it comes to something like this. I don't understand it because when she and I and the girls had that apartment on Bleecker, who do you think *made* the place? If she didn't have a date, or a class at the New School, she'd get out the Dutch oven your mother gave her and make gallons of oxtail soup, all according to your mother's recipe. I swear, the kitchen looked like one of those produce stands you see along the road in Jersey. Vegetables all over the place, and then the pounds of oxtails all cut up in two-, three-, four- and five-inch pieces, depending on the circumference of each piece. But did we love the soup, and did it come in handy at the end of the month when we were all broke."

"She was right, though, wasn't she, to have no confidence? With the bastard she picked, she was right. Look at this place. All right, she's no interior decorator, but you can tell she tried." He went over to a commode where he had seen an opened bottle of Scotch. "I was about to say the Jew bastard she picked."

"But you're a lapsed Catholic, so you didn't. I know. You can't be lapsed and anti-Semitic too." She was just trying to break him down, get him out of it, but it was no use. Oona had always been his favorite, and here, amidst her rush-order plans and hopes, he couldn't help lashing out at Friedensohn.

"Listen," he said, and poured some Scotch in a couple of glasses. As strong and tough as when he had played football, he looked even stronger and tougher when angry. "I've never hated a Jew before, and I don't like being unable to hate him as I should, as I *want* to hate him. I mean why should phoniness creep into my feelings against this Friedensohn bastard? Or against any other Jew bastard, for that matter? I can hate all other bastards—Irish bastards especially—until the cows come home. Sure, okay. But a Jew bastard? A Negro or a Puerto Rican bastard? No. And you know why? 'Transition.' We're living in 'transition,' you see, so before I hate a Jew bastard, or a Negro or Puerto Rican bastard, I'm supposed to look into my motives, analyze myself, check and recheck until I wind up being the bastard. The only trouble with that horseshit is this. Transition is here to stay and I'm not. And neither are all the bastards who are slipping by now without being properly hated because they belong to some goddamn minority. I'll be up to my hips in the grave and I'll still be living in transition. Sure, the minorities may be different then, but what good will that do me? It'll still be transition, won't it? I'll still be expected to phony up my feelings to keep the thing going, won't I? At least in Limbo, goddamn it, there's no hope of ever reaching heaven."

He stopped to sip his drink, but gulped the whole thing down instead. Nancy knew, doctor friends of theirs had told her, that he was tactful and kind in his dealings with the sick. How hard to think that now, though. Jim had been a stutterer all through grammar and high school, and now—could he pump the old words out now. Nancy did not make a study of her husband so much as allow him to come into existence in her mind. Nor did she submit these impressions to inner scrutiny, willing as she was to let life "go at that" in order to live it. She had given up expecting an answer to every question. Life was to be lived, not understood, and lived continuously, by the device of acceptance. So Jim had been a stutterer and now he pumped the old words out. So what? He wasn't a stutterer any more, that's what mattered to Nancy—the anymore part.

"I don't mean I'm against progress," Jim was saying. "Only where do you go if you're not thrilled by being *for* the Negro, *for* the Jew, *for* the Puerto Rican—and not thrilled for the simple reason that it never occurred to you to be against them in the first place? You don't go anywhere. There's no place *to* go. You belong to a different kind of minority, the one minority no one gives a damn about. And you know why? No political action committee, no Washington pressure group, no meetings, no dues, no leader. A bigot who hates a Jew is one thing. I just didn't think I'd be bothered too. I'd be the one person, I always thought, who'd hate a Jew—you know, with ease. Nothing phony. All right, here's my own sister and what this rotten bastard has done to her, and what happens? I can't hate him. I don't feel right hating him."

"Don't you *know* you're not anti-Semitic? If you know, and you *know* you're not, Jim, why aren't you free to feel any way you want?"

"I'll tell you why. Because part of me moonlights now as an anti-bigot. I can't hear the uninterrupted music of my hatred for Friedensohn because this moonlighter, you see, this phony liberal inside me, keeps dropping names in my ear. NAACP, American Jewish Committee, Anti-Defamation League, and so on. 'I know it's your sister,' he keeps whispering, 'but Friedensohn's Jewish, right? So use caution. Be a little ashamed you hate him. Wonder about it. Ask yourself questions. Suspect yourself.' "

"Do you hate Friedensohn because he's Jewish or because of what he's done to Oona?"

"I *want* to hate him because of what he's done to

Oona, but I can't because he's Jewish."

"Oh, God, Jim, call Friedensohn a bastard, will you? Call him anything, only get it over with before Oona comes back. She's having the baby by him, not you."

"What do you want me to do, Nancy, *like* Friedensohn?"

"No, I want you to like Oona. Hate Friedensohn now. Hate him all you want now. But when Oona comes home, don't hate him. Like Oona and her baby. That's what she's going to want you to do. That's what she's going to need."

"You crazy—" There were tears in his eyes. "Did I say it was going to take that long to hate him?"

Suddenly, with a bang, the door flew open and a small but blustery man rushed in with a baseball bat and the determination to use it. He had obviously expected to find teen-agers from First Avenue, an errant delivery boy who knew the Friedensohns were away, possibly seasoned burglars, and considering the age (about sixty-five) and size (about five feet four inches) of the man, it took courage indeed to try to save the day armed only with a bat and a featherweight's brawn. He was all limbs, like a puppet, despite his diminutive size, with a head, large only in comparison with the rest of his body, that grew like a scallion out of a stiff collar high enough to prevent the stem, or neck, from showing, and the chin from falling. Theatrical was the word for the man, so much so that Jim thought, was positive, he was wearing makeup. His eyebrows were much blacker than his hair, and the eyes themselves were outlined in black, with telltale dots of black in the corners where the pencil had apparently skipped over the wrinkled skin. There was a suggestion of bay rum, of five-and-ten talc and unguent for the hair, of the lips having been outlined against the aging, powdery skin with a wet finger or a moistened bit of cotton. No doubt of it, he was an old theater man, a run-down vaudevillian out for a "breather" while the talkie was on.

"Who are you and what are you doing here?" he said, his pronunciation self-consciously correct, his voice well thrown so that those in the last row could hear him. It was a good performance except that the scene, a young man and woman sipping Scotch, did not call for such vehemence. He lowered the bat, but tried hard not to lower his determination.

"Mr. McManus?" Jim said, slipping the authorization from the inside pocket of his jacket. "My name is James O'Hagen, and this is my wife."

The man smiled as if by rote, as if introductions, to no matter whom, required that he be civil.

"My sister," Jim went on, "Oona O'Hagen—that is, Mrs. Friedensohn—asked us to come here on an errand. She sent us the keys from Europe, and this authorization, notarized at the American Express office in Florence."

(49)

The authorization quickly read, the man's face, manner and even posture changed. A looseness at the hips, coupled with a tendency to bend forward from the waist, like a tap dancer doing a difficult step, made him seem even smaller than he was. He broke into a wrinkled smile that made him temporarily more Chinese than Irish. "Ah, Mr. O'Hagen, why didn't you come directly to me? I *am* McManus and your sister is a grand person, a pleasure to talk to, a joy to behold. The doctor I met only once, but once is enough. The man's a gentleman from his widow's peak downward, 'a movie star,' as your own sister put it, 'with an M.D.' "

"Will you have a drink with us, Mr. McManus?"

"Ah, thank you, Mr. O'Hagen. But I mustn't. I have enough trouble leveling off the elevator as it is. But thank you. Thank you just the same. Thank you," he went on, smiling too broadly and bowing too low, his dependence on liquor showing through his excessive civility now he was sober. Behind the appreciative smiles, the attentiveness, and the ready disposition to yield was a genuine concern about himself—the fear that to disrupt the amenities now would be to jeopardize his chances for a pleasant jingle later. Whiskey was a god whose guardianship might be withheld if he raised his voice, or quarreled, or revealed his desperate need of it, in any way. He glanced down at the bottle with something like familiarity. Had he slipped into the apartment now and then, taken nips from that same bottle while the Friedensohns were away? If so, he was in the clear; the bottle's depletion would now be attributed to the brother and sister-in-law.

"I insist," Jim said, more for Oona's sake, for good relations, for whatever useful information the man might give him, than for the man himself. He poured a healthy double ounce into a glass and, with that overriding insistence so appreciated by drinkers on the receiving end, made McManus take it.

"But what's this about the furniture?" McManus said, his first sip taken. "All this lovely furniture Mrs. Friedensohn couldn't see enough of, nor talk enough about. Every day another carton or package would come, and I'd help her open it, help her stuff the wrappings down the incinerator. Now they're not coming back?"

Jim said not as soon as expected, that his sister was ill and had decided in any case to remain in Europe for another six months, perhaps a year. Meanwhile, she wanted them to have the lease voided and the furniture moved to Lincoln Warehouse.

"This is serious," McManus said. "Serious. It's very serious," he went on, as though nothing at 84 Irving Place were serious but trying to have a lease voided. "The landlord, you see, is strictly a lease man. Hotelier. Managed the old Cadillac on 43rd

Street back during prohibition when half the bellhops were unemployed actors." Beneath each eye,
as he smiled, there appeared a pinch of skin like a
clothespin mark. "Bing Crosby was across the street
at the Paramount, held over so long they had to
keep changing the picture. You two don't remember, you're too young. But they'd darken the theater,
put a spot on Bing, and send him out over the
audience on this crane sort of thing that opened out
like a telescope. He'd move slowly back and forth in
the pitch-darkness, singing a medley, and when he
hovered, I'm telling you, when that man hovered,
those girls squealed! You talk about Sinatra . . ."

He stopped again, and the clothespin smile re-
appeared. The man was perhaps twice removed
from the derelict they had just passed in the street,
though he still had his faculties, his memories, his
little reaches for the unrecoverable.

"The landlord, though, the landlord. Yes. Well,
now, he's the Conrad Hilton of run-down apartment houses. Buys them up, renovates them
on a shoestring, gets a turnover of tenants, and
a new file of leases. You go to his office, and
you're going to have to if you want the lease voided,
you'll see a motto on the wall. 'In a hotel,' it says,
'a card on every guest. In an apartment house, a
lease for every tenant.' He wrote it himself and had
it painted on one of those Home-Sweet-Home
pieces of wood. Lives up to it, too. Right up—all

the way. I know the man."

"Is he a Jew?" Jim said, and blushed at how prepared he was to resent the landlord on the assumption that another Jew bastard had crossed his path. If only an Irishman had done this to Oona, he could hate him naturally, as he did his own brother Kevin. There would be no need to go underground this way with his feelings, and therefore no desire to blame other Irishmen for what one Irishman had done. But Friedensohn was a Jew, and so his hatred for him was already entangled with his guilt—that vast, amorphous Hitler guilt from which no Christian could escape. Which only made it worse, since for every Jew bastard he didn't hate openly, he would hate a dozen non-bastard Jews secretly.

McManus had picked up Oona's First Holy Communion prayer book and begun to shake his head sadly at the image of Christ on the Cross. In a thick, authentic-sounding brogue, he said, " 'Whin we luck at him there, we see our blissed Saviour, stripped a'most naked lake ourselves; whin we luck at the crown o' thorns on the head, we see the Jews mockin' him, jist the same as—some people mock ourselves for our religion; whin we luck at his eyes, we see they wor niver dry, like our own; whin we luck at the wound at his side, why, we think less of our own wounds an' bruises, we get 'ithin and 'ithout every day av our lives.' "

"What do you mean by that, Mr. McManus? Say what you mean," Jim said. His whole face had become blotched with anger. Was Oona's prayer book the cause of it all? Could that little gold image of Christ crucified, coupled with his hatred for Friedensohn, have touched some deep chord within him that perhaps all Christians shared? "You can't be lapsed and anti-Semitic too," Nancy had said. Of course she'd been joking, but what about the reverse of what she'd said? Could she unwittingly have touched upon some kind of crucifixion curse that made it almost impossible for a Christian not to be anti-Semitic? How many times as a boy had he been told by the nuns at Corpus Christi Church that the Jews had crucified Christ? And while he was being told that, how many Jews were playing on the same sandlot football team with him? At least five. All that time, could he have been an anti-Semite without knowing it? Did he know now? Would he ever know? Would Andy Cohen, who played on the same football team and later went to N.Y.U., know where *he* stood if an Irishman had done this to his sister?

"I gave that little speech on a stage in Boston forty years ago," McManus was saying. "I still remember it, still remember the applause I got from the Irish in the audience." He gulped down the rest of his drink and went on. "Ah, Mr. O'Hagen, forgive an old man, but don't be against your sister's marriage because the man's a Jew. They're in love, those two—"

"I'm not against the marriage, Mr. McManus, I'm sorry I gave you that impression." He was being false and self-righteous and he knew it. He didn't know what he was against, or for. He just wished Oona would stop getting into trouble all the time.

"Good, then. Good!" McManus said. "And I'm sorry I misunderstood you. As for the landlord, no, he's not a Jew. He's a Greek, if you want to know the truth, his name notwithstanding. John Strickland, he calls himself. A Greek with an English name."

"Well, look. About the lease," Jim said, the blood slowly leaving his face. "Everything in the kitchen was installed at the Friedensohns' expense. The landlord could have those appliances—the stove, refrigerator, and sink. They're all new. Never been used."

"That should help considerably, Mr. O'Hagen, if you use the right approach, and the right approach is to keep calling him Strickland. He loves that, loves to be introduced to people. Loves to introduce himself to people. 'Strickland's the name,' he'll say. 'Strick-land.' His real name, Vaselin, is what did it, I think. That, and the bellhops pronouncing it with an 'e' at the end. 'Mr. Vaseline,' they called him. And then, when he put on all the weight, the same game, only worse. 'Petroleum Jelly' it became. 'Mr.

Petroleum' for short. Ah, it was a shame the way
they had the greenhorn chambermaids calling him
Mr. Petroleum to his face. 'Good morning to you,
Mr. Petroleum,' they'd say in the corridors. All
innocence, until the poor man began to wonder
who he was. And so John Strickland it became. A
second christening, the bellhops called it, and that
it was." He put his glass down and prepared to
leave. "Ah, and don't let my little speech before
make you think I'm against the Irish, Mr. O'Hagen.
You can say what you want about them, but from
the first brick thrown, they fought for their rights
out of court, where rights are really won. They
fought at the factory gates, in the railroad yards, on
the docks, until those Irish Need Not Apply signs
came down. And now look at us. Why, if the
archdiocese were to move into the Pentagon tomorrow, I wouldn't so much as flick an eye. Believe me,
I wouldn't."

"Tell me, Mr. McManus, how did you know we
were here?"

McManus put his finger to his lips and pointed to
the wall, beyond which, apparently, was the next
apartment. "Widow," he whispered, still sweet with
the capacity to enjoy life's insignificant wonders.
"Very interested in your sister and her husband. A
regular ferret. I would never have known you were
here. She works at night. But this is her night
off."

CHAPTER IV

On May 12th Oona took the "feeler bus" to Florence to see about a package that her sister Cathy had promised to have Macy's airmail to her, and returned home to Fiesole at about 11 P.M. It was one of those cold drizzly nights when even a Kleenex feels wet, and by the time she got home that is what she might have been wearing—a wet Kleenex with a scalloped hem. Her yellow voile. She should never have worn anything so flimsy, but it had been sunny when she left, and the bouffant skirt, which still fit her around the waist, had complimented her pregnancy.

Worse by far than the dress, though, was that the maid, at her mother's all day with lumbago, had forgotten to leave wood for a fire. It was so cold and everything felt so sticky that at first Oona couldn't believe the bin was empty. She went closer to make sure, and when there wasn't even any kindling, she thought of America and of what a fire you could make in a pinch with a single copy of the Sunday *New York Times*. Her every thought on the way home had been of the fireplace, and now here it was, like a liquor store a minute after closing time. She started out to try to get some wood herself, but remembering how she'd both perspired and had chills on the way home, she decided instead to heat water for a bath.

Afterward, sitting in the kitchen in a nightgown, sweater and robe, she felt much better. She always nibbled on something at night when she read, and that was what she was doing, nibbling on bread and cheese and sipping milk with cognac in it, when the labor pains started.

She sat there, anger like a compress against her temples, as the first attack subsided. For she had had false labor before, and though there had been nothing false about the pain, she was more annoyed than frightened. Even when the attacks grew worse and she began taking the cognac straight, she discounted the danger of actually giving birth without help. Just the same, she got towels and a basin of water and lots of pots spilling with water and brought her clock from the bedroom to time the intervals between attacks. They had been coming about every fifteen minutes and were now, at two-thirty, coming every ten. Finally, when they began coming every eight minutes, she did some quick mental arithmetic. It was already after three, but even so, at this rate, if the labor was genuine (and she was beginning to think it was), she would have the baby before the maid arrived—if with lumbago the maid arrived at all.

Standing up from the table, she made her way to the front door before the next attack started. She gripped the doorframe to brace herself against the pain, then, as it subsided, opened the door and began ringing a large bell (similar to a cowbell) that she had bought in Florence for when she took her long afternoon bath and the maid was out hanging laundry. She'd called from the bathroom during her first false alarm and the maid hadn't heard her, so after buying the bell she'd told the maid, "Maria, if you ever hear this bell"—and she rang it—"wherever you are and whatever you're doing, come immediately. I'll only ring it if I really need you."

Of course she knew that Maria was at her mother's over a mile away, but one of the things about being an American in a small Italian town was that you were talked about. Maria might have told her friends about her mistress's "cowbell," and they in turn might have told others. But even as Oona rang it, even as she went on ringing it, she realized that Tony on their arrival had purposely (romantically) chosen the most secluded villa in Fiesole, and that at four in the morning in the rain there would not be a soul near the place.

Was it a trick she was playing on herself? Had she come to Italy this way, broke and pregnant, with a weak, irresolute man, in some crazy attempt to outdo her mother who had had all seven children at home but none without a doctor's help? Her mother's heart was even supposed to have stopped for a minute after Jim was born, but that hadn't discouraged her mother. Blood, bruises, stitches, broken bones—nothing had ever bothered Maggie O'Hagen so long as the blood flowed, the stitches were sewn in, and the bones were set, at home. In a hospital—no, not the same thing at all. The hospital bed and nurses and the smells and regulations were all so unfamiliar that your own blood became unfamiliar. Whereas at home blood was blood. You saw the familiar cracks in the ceiling, went back over the stories they told, asked for some tea and knew it would be made in a pot as familiar as your own hand. At home—no doubt of it—even dying would be easy for her mother. "Don't forget the laundry," she would probably say as she closed her eyes for good, "the beds need changing."

As another attack started, a strange thing happened to Oona. She half looked at herself in the alcove mirror, and whether it was because she looked so unusual, crouched over with the bell in her hand, or because the pain was so intense, she saw herself with imagination, she became objective to herself. At the same time she could not have felt sorrier for herself (the person she knew she was) if she had been somebody else. Her leg and neck muscles were working in a way that she would have thought possible only in a man. Her stance, too, was pigeon-toed, though she wasn't. Some esthetic ambiguity made her at once a powerful man and the most poignantly beautiful of women. She loved herself at that moment exactly as Father Monahan had once exhorted her—along with all the other parishioners of Corpus Christi Church—to love others. Recalling those sermons of his, she wondered why he had never said anything about loving yourself as though you were somebody else, and others as though they were you. Because you couldn't love others unless they were you, or yourself unless you were somebody else. She hadn't lost her mind—on the contrary, what amazed her, quietly, like an opening in the pain, was that she hadn't thought of it before.

She had no idea when it happened, the exact time in the morning, that is, but suddenly she felt an urge "to go" and rushed to the bathroom. She remembered dropping the bell on the slate floor and the wrong kind of sound it made as the real final pain caught her and she doubled over. She was down in a squatting position with the sweat pouring off her and burning into her eyes, and that's how she delivered the baby, almost dropping it, on the floor. It screamed and urinated all over her, a girl so small and wretched that she started to cry. They were still attached and she was afraid she might kill the baby by falling on it from loss of blood or by trying to cut and tie the umbilical cord herself. At the same time, as though succumbing to importunity itself, she began to give the baby's screams more and more attention. She had never heard the little voice before, and what she was doing, unwittingly, was allowing the mere sound of it to divert her attention from her real plight, which was beyond doing anything about anyway. Even when the screaming stopped and she had nothing to distract her, she felt too weak to do anything without help.

So after covering the baby with some towels, she sat on the toilet with the baby on her lap and started ringing the bell again. Whenever she stopped to rest she could feel the umbilical cord throbbing against her thigh. She could *see* it throbbing. It was still alive and that was why she kept ringing the bell—to "keep the kettle boiling" (the words of that childhood game actually passed through her mind) until help came. The maid wasn't due for over an hour, but it was beginning to grow light and she thought the milk woman or some farmer or passing tourist might hear it. But no one came. There were no footsteps or passing cars—no sounds at all except those from the leaky water tap in the room with her.

She sat there a long time. The room's low, cold air kept crowding round her ankles, but she sat there, she didn't know why except that no better idea occurred to her. She was there, so she tended to remain there, and after a while, when she forgot she was waiting for someone to come, when, indeed, it would have been easier to believe no one was ever going to come again, the stillness underwent the same second growth that it does in cathedrals and cemeteries and among ruins. She had walked into the Duomo of St. Mary of the Flower in Florence one afternoon, and after a while, after the fresh outside air had emanated from her clothes, and the pew had become familiar and homelike, something other than the stillness of the place, something like the stillness but not the stillness itself, had been added.

The same kind of other thing was happening to the stillness now, only this time she wasn't paying attention, she really didn't care. She began to care less and less, in fact. It was easier just to sit there and not care about anything at all, or do anything at all. Even after she realized she was passing out from loss of blood, she still tended to remain where she was because that's where she was. She didn't *want* to die, but it was so much easier to die than to get up that she instinctively, at the last minute, chose the harder course and got up.

Though bleeding badly and so dizzy that the house might have been a boat, she carried the baby, still attached to her and as slippery as a fish, to the bedroom where she laid it on the bed. Birds were beginning to sing around the house and she could no longer hear the rain. "It's stopped raining," she said aloud, she didn't know why. Never in her life had she felt so cold and damp *inside* a house. Her teeth were chattering and she was shaking all over. She couldn't stop, and she *had* to stop, because when she stepped to the dresser to get the scissors, she took up all the slack in the umbilical cord. The scissors were in either the left or right top drawer, but since she could just barely reach the dresser as it was, she could only open the left and they weren't *in* the left. She didn't want to uncover and lift the slippery baby again, but neither did she feel strong enough to draw the dresser closer. So there she was, as close to the dresser as the cord would allow, but not close enough to get the scissors. She looked at the baby, at herself, at the connecting cord between them, and felt almost literally in two different places at the same time. Finally she went back to the bed—there was nothing else *to* do—and lifted the baby to bring it over to the dresser. The cord between them went slack and she got the most vivid feeling that *she* wasn't on the bed any more.

The baby's not crying then was a godsend, for when she got the scissors, the silence made it easier for her to control herself and make a note of things. She could hold her movements up to view, so to speak, and in that way become what she was doing, a single, operating unit. She put the baby back on the bed and tied the cord in two places with ribbons from her nightgown. Then, with a momentary thought for the baby that was like a prayer, she cut the cord between the two tied places.

By now the baby was so blue and cold that she thought it was dead. She put her ear against its chest, which was all heart and thumping away, and lay down herself. The sun had come up and was making little inquiries at the window, and as she lay there, watchful in a lazy, off and on way, it was a comfort to have to consider that there was a chance of the baby's wetting her again. It was good to lie in bed next to a baby who might wet you. She remembered how, in parochial school, she used to promise God something if He did what she asked. Saying it was good to lie in bed was like promising God something, only this time she didn't know, she didn't *want* to know, what she was asking.

A few scrappy thoughts about cotton and gauze came to mind before she closed her eyes, but exhaustion, on top of the feeling of being *consoled* in some way, had made her, at the same time, enormously indifferent. The birth would perhaps mean something tomorrow; it meant nothing now. That she had been through it meant something, that the baby and she had, as it were, won. She had changed in some important way but she didn't know how yet. She didn't have to know. The change would be there for her, waiting for her, when she caught up with it.

She fell asleep and was wakened by the milk woman taking away the empties. Italians had a

thing about noise, Oona thought, and if she was
right, that they used noise, lots of noise, as company
when they were alone, or as a signal to others that
they didn't want to be alone, then her milk woman
was a gregarious person living a hermit's life. Oona
had been annoyed by the woman from the day she
had arrived at the villa, but now, suddenly, nothing
could have been more welcome than the sound of
those rattling empties. She grabbed the bell and
started ringing it. But how many times in New York
had she turned up her hi-fi to drown out a noisy
neighbor? What if the woman thought she was just
trying to drown her out? She stopped ringing and
listened, and the woman was making more noise
than ever, so she started shouting to her in Italian
that she was alone and needed help, that the
woman should come in, come in, come in!

It was darker in the room than it was outside, and
when the woman first scuffed over the threshold,
she just peered at Oona with her head to one side
and her nose twisted. She saw Oona and the bell,
that is, but not the baby, and seemed to think the
young American had lost her mind. Oona had to lift
the covers from around the baby's head and show
her, which was a mistake (she should have tried to
tell her), for when the woman saw the baby's messy
little face she let out a scream such as you would
hear only in a country like Italy, where the people
still walked their dead to the cemetery and there

were ruins almost as old as the land itself and even the street cleaners were addicted to opera. It was a scream filled with such pity and terror that Oona was suddenly struck by the thought that no one had forced her to have her baby in Italy. This revelation had the startling effect of making her think it was still possible to have the baby in France. At that moment, as the thought of an alternative country crossed her mind, Oona must have looked as crazy to the woman as the woman looked to Oona, for suddenly the woman, raising both hands to her head as though her hair had caught fire, ran out screaming. Oona started after her, to tell her what to do, where to go, but after the first few steps the house began to capsize, and in an effort to right herself she tried to stand on the ceiling.

She came to on the floor as a doctor arrived from Fiesole. Either the milk woman had told a confused story, or the doctor, being Italian himself, had made allowances for exaggeration. He carried Oona to the bedroom and laid her—almost on top of the baby— on the bed. He did not know, that is, or believe, that she had already had the baby, and when she showed him, and he saw the ribbons, he didn't lose his head, he became—there was no other word for it—*triumphant*, a much larger and more expansive man. First, in a very deep baritone voice, he said, "Ah!" Then, swaggering back and forth with the most wonderful play of emotions, Oona thought, around

his eyes and mouth, he kept saying, "Instinct!
Instinct! Instinct!" as though by cutting the cord
herself she had freed *him* of something. He was
triumphant, Oona thought, in a nice way, the way
the French were when Lindbergh landed. She and
the baby might have been dying, of course, but as
things turned out she was glad the doctor acted as
he did. She would always remember that part of it
because he seemed, well, pure, as though he'd just
come into the world himself.

Meanwhile, five Italian women were cleaning the
baby and wrapping her in gauze and cotton in the
kitchen. They kept laughing and talking among
themselves, and whenever the doctor joined them
for a moment, to get something he'd been steriliz-
ing, they always tried to draw him into their discus-
sion, which had to do with what they called the
baby's perfection—her long blonde hair, long fingers, and high, noble brow. Oona, in the bedroom,
didn't catch everything they said, but the doctor
knew how to turn the sharp, slangy corners to their
hearts, because the laughter always increased while
he was there. It might have been an Italian feast
day, the way they were acting, and what Oona
liked was that the fun was at no one's expense.

Finally, after the doctor had removed the afterbirth and given Oona countless stitches, after he'd
told her how brave she was and how much he
admired her (he was a great believer in instinct and

she didn't have the heart to tell him that Tony
Friedensohn had told her all about how the umbilical cord was tied), he asked for permission to give
the story, with pictures of Oona and the baby, to
the newspapers. Ordinarily Oona would have loved
the fanfare and excitement, but she realized that
under the circumstances it wouldn't be wise to
answer questions, let alone to allow pictures. Quite
aside from Mrs. Friedensohn and the trouble she
might cause, Oona could just imagine her mother
and father's reaction to seeing her, and a grandchild
they didn't even know existed, in the New York
Daily News. All the same, news of the birth had
everybody in Fiesole sending gauze, cotton, linen,
powder and alcohol, and soon the villa became
more tourist attraction than home. English and
American residents came by to inquire, and every
day Oona saw curious Italians pass.

Two weeks went by before Oona felt strong
enough to write a letter. She was determined to
breast-feed her baby (her mother had breast-fed all
seven children) and that took all her strength. The
baby's other needs were no problem, though, for on
the day of the birth, before the five Italian women
had even finished in the kitchen, Oona's maid
returned wearing a new dress and new pride in the
Villa Roseto and its tenants and said she would
shop, cook and take care of Oona and the baby
herself. The Fiesole doctor who had come to Oona's

aid, Dr. Elio Maderini, an elderly man with a huge bathrobe of a body, a red tweedy face that he seemed almost to think with, and a soft baritone voice that insinuated itself past all kinds of barriers, dropped by once and sometimes even twice a day to see Oona, who began to think of his second visit on any given day as her consolation prize. He spoke much better English than she spoke Italian and acted almost from the start (and this amazed and delighted her) as though he had known her all his life. He liked her company and she liked his. They were both demonstrative, and since he kept worrying about Oona's failure to put on weight, he saved Oona the trouble of worrying about it.

On May 25, when Oona did feel strong enough to sit up, she wrote Jim and Nancy a very long letter about what had happened. She told them everything she remembered or had been told about the birth, but the trouble was, having by then grown used to the details, she related them as though Jim and Nancy were used to them too. This made the letter much more shocking to Jim and Nancy than an emotionally written letter would have been, for in reading it they had to do all the work, drum up all the emotion, themselves. Jim found the part near the end, which touched only incidentally on the birth itself, the most shocking of all, for it was not only filled with gossipy feminine details, but written as though the birth *were* incidental. It was the part where Oona, suddenly finished with the birth (which Jim, a doctor, naturally wanted to know more about), went on to say:

At this point, could I ask you to do me a favor —another, I mean? I have diapers, pants, night-gowns, shirts, towels, and blankets, and I will have, soon, a cradle, and a basin for her bath. But could you slip two blue plastic bibs in an envelope (they'll weigh very little) and send them to me air-mail? She drools a lot and I really need them, and in Florence they're all made of fine embroidered linen or silk.

About the apartment. I sent McManus $50 to buy a second-hand trunk for my things, and what they came in were two suitcases dating back to the potato-famine of 1850. If not for the butchers' twine he'd reinforced them with (they had no handles), they would have fallen apart. Then he sent the three gray rugs, which I didn't want, and the white rug for the bathroom, which I did want, but not the toilet-seat cover to match. Two sheets and two pillow cases are missing. Are they in the hamper? He forgot to send the pillows themselves (I guess you know that), and two white blouses are missing and some towels. But more important—the silverware should have six of everything, and one knife and two teaspoons are missing. Are they there? Everytime I look for something, I discover something else missing. I know (think) he's honest, so I'm confused. As it is, they're holding the radio in Genoa until I return.

Will you let me know about the above? Because everything is insured and I could perhaps collect. Please write soon.

Love,

OONA O'

CHAPTER V

In the dining room where for years she had cut out so many dress patterns for her daughters that the dry-goods smell still lingered, Maggie O'Hagen sat musing over a cup of tea. She was alone, and the quiet house, the canary's perky industry, the dampened laundry rolled in balls for ironing, the spreading stain of moisture in the newspaper under the philodendron plants, the fire-escape-filtered sunlight on her arms were all part of a morning so beyond questioning and yet so instinctively felt that it was as if last year were this year, yesterday today. Tea brewed in a scalded pot with leaves dug from the canister and "weighed" in the hand: she drank nothing else, and indeed mused over nothing else, so that at times it was hard to tell which gave her the satisfaction, the tea in her cup or the leaves at the bottom.

Cathy's early day, no afternoon classes, she thought. She'll be home wanting something to eat.

Pushing herself up from the table, she took her

cup and saucer with her and padded back through
the apartment in what the family called her "uni-
form"—a bandanna cut from leftover dress material,
the blue-and-white canvas shoes she always wore at
home, and, over a slip trimmed with lace, an
unbuttoned cardigan whose pockets, stuffed with
receipts, recipes, hairpins, rosary beads, pencil stubs,
and spools of thread, fell away from the faint rise of
her stomach as she walked.

In the kitchen she got a glass dish from the
refrigerator and lifted it uncovered to her nose.
Then, always a great one for low lights, she put a
low light under a saucepan and dropped in some
butter, wiping it clean off the spoon with her
thumb. When it started to melt, she made three
separate piles in the pan with what was in the glass
dish: one meat, one mashed potatoes, and the third
string beans. The meat, in chunks, looked whitish
here and there where the gravy had hardened, but it
wasn't in the pan long before it began to look tender
and brown and juicy. She covered it, and on top of
the cover she put two leftover biscuits, and while it
simmered along, she got out a fresh bottle of milk
and some pound cake.

She made so little noise as she worked that the
food might have come out of a sack she carried
around with her. She never wasted herself with
nervous, jerky movements, and for her children

there had always been something soothing, almost hypnotic, in watching her baste a hem or dust the furniture or even mop a floor. She created the illusion of doing everything slowly, without exerting herself, and was never so content as when her hands were dipping and swirling over some task.

Suddenly her favorite sound, the telephone ringing, sent her to the living room, to the chair by the window overlooking the Hudson River, her favorite window, next to which the telephone table stood.

"It's not really you, Jim, is it?" she said.

"What's that for, Ma?"

"You never drop by to see me any more."

"What are you talking about? I dropped by two weeks ago."

"You dropped by a month ago. Two miles away and I see you—what, five times a year? Wait'll I'm gone."

"Where're you going?"

"Don't be funny, Jim. I mean it."

"Oh, cut it out, you big phony. Nancy and I have asked you out a hundred times."

"Wait a minute. There's a light on the stove."

Jim could hear the receding pad-pad-pad of her feet as she walked away. He was in a telephone booth and he hated telephone booths, so while waiting he reread Oona's latest letter, which he had found in his box on his way to the hospital that morning.

Fiesole, Firenze, Italy
June 3, 1953

Dear Jim & Nancy,

How I appreciate having you two on that side of
the Atlantic! Every night for weeks I've lain awake
thinking of that apartment and of what I'd do if you
couldn't get the furniture stored in Lincoln. And
you say the landlord inspected the paint job, accepted the new stove, sink and refrigerator, and
voided the lease without protest? Good for Moral
Rearmament. As for McManus, how well I know
he's a character. He used to be a song and dance
man, and one afternoon, in my living room, gave me
a demonstration that was hysterical.

In my last letter I forgot to emphasize that not a
word about the birth is for family consumption.
Mama will have enough to worry about if anything
happens to Papa, whose "minor" heart attack last
year might have been one of those occult major
ones. Everybody keeps forgetting that he has very
little insurance, no pension, and, except for the
business, no assets.

Up to now I've never given "insurance" a second
thought, but now I have a daughter and that
afternoon in the villa with Tony and his wife keeps
coming back to plague me. Just today I received a
note from Mrs. Friedensohn saying that she and
Tony had learned of the circumstances of the birth
and that they were both very sorry. "I wish now that

you would give some thought to my offer," she said. "You are so young. Your life is only beginning."

When you consider it's only been three weeks since I've *had* the baby, don't you think she should have waited a bit before showing me how intelligently she handles *her* affairs?

Tony—and I'm sure without her knowledge—sent flowers "with love and great admiration." All right, that was decent. He didn't send money because he knows I wouldn't accept it. I mean he knows *me*, the bastard, so the flowers *were* nice, they really were. He wasn't thinking of himself or his rights to the baby, he was thinking of me.

In my letter to Cathy I told her to give you the family's old mags if you don't have any. I'm dying to see a Sunday Times, *The New Yorker*, *Esquire*—anything that would really *put* me in New York, and, for an hour at least, *keep* me there. It's crazy, but I miss that Village apartment you and I and the girls used to have, Nancy. I miss the New School and those novel-writing seminars and all the never-to-be-published novels. One, I remember, began with the hero slipping off the stern of an ocean liner in the middle of the night. By the time a Norwegian freighter picked him up, twelve hours later, he'd given himself a depth interview to the tune of about 900 pages. I even miss the man who wrote it, a thin intense fellow with library eyes and the greatest willingness to share *your* problems as a "writer." I also miss the beautiful Chinese children coming out of Transfiguration Parochial School on Mott Street, and the men poking through the bins of hardware along Canal (a possible use for this, a definite need for that).

The days are so lovely now and the lovelier they are the lonelier I feel. Write soon, and remember, "A slip of the lip may sink a ship."

Love,

OONA O'

Jim slipped the letter back in his pocket. He had called his mother to feel her out about Oona, had purposely not dropped by, that is, for fear that in her presence he might give something away. Maggie O'Hagen could "see through" her children, she thought, and more often than not she was right. Her very first question on returning to the phone, in fact, made Jim smile.

"Have you heard from Oona?"

"Not recently. Why?"

"Jim, why do you always do this when I ask you about Oona? I'm her mother. Don't you think I should be told if anything's wrong? Don't you think I have a right to know?"

"What have I done? You asked me if I'd heard from Oona and I said not recently. I don't get you, Madame Olga, no kidding. Did you read something in your tea leaves this morning, or have you heard from her?"

"Jim, don't think I don't know when you're beating around the bush, so don't try it."

Slowly going deaf, she had begun to listen to him when he wasn't talking and hear what he made a point of not saying. If instead of telephoning he had dropped by, she would be peering into his face now, touching his arm, grasping with some almost tactile sense the suggestion that something was wrong. The telephone was safer, for though she used it hours every day to call her daughters, the butcher, and the bookie who took her bets, though it had become her "secret" hearing aid, it weakened her instinctive prowess, her Madame Olga insights, if only because it was an aid and a mechanical one at that. Only when her children were there in front of her, when, ironically, many of the things they said were lost, did she get the messages that enabled her to see through them.

"Ma, will you please tell me what you've heard? If I had heard from her, you'd want me to tell you, wouldn't you?"

"You really haven't heard from her, Jim? Honest?"

"No! Now will you tell me?"

"She's adopted a child in Italy."

"She's *what?*" Oona not only made you lie, she not only complicated your life and left an endless wake of confusion behind her, she even made you a ham actor.

"Jim, the way you say that. Come over and let me look at you, Jim."

"Ma, I knew you were going to say that. I swear, clairvoyance must be hereditary. You read tea leaves, and I know what you're going to say before you say it."

"Jim, are you coming over?"

"Of course not. I'm meeting Nancy downtown in an hour. How can I come over?"

"You're afraid to come over. You knew about the adoption."

"Ma, that's one thing I didn't know. Honest."

"Then it isn't true. If you didn't know, it isn't true. You and Nancy get everything first. I'm her mother, but you two get everything first. I knew there was something crazy about that story."

"Listen, Olga, listen! I'm not calling from home. I'm calling from a telephone booth on 72nd Street. There may be a letter from Oona in our box right now, for all I know. Maybe she wrote both of us more or less the same letter. Did she say why she adopted a child? How old is the child, anyway?" Hollywood, he thought, here I come.

"It's an infant, and she adopted it because the mother, her cook, she said, died the day it was born. What I'd like to know is, what was Oona doing with a cook?"

"In Italy it doesn't mean that much to have a cook, Ma. What you pay to have your windows cleaned every month, that's what you'd pay for a cook in Italy."

"Eight dollars a month for a cook?"

"The cook eats too, you know."

"You're lying, Jim. There's something wrong about all this, and I'm going to find out what it is. You know what's wrong, but you won't tell me."

"Double the cook's salary, for goodness sake. All right? Triple it. Make it an even twenty-five dollars a month. Is that a lot to pay for a cook? But I'm telling you, Ma, that's about what you'd pay for one in Italy."

"If you can't come over today, Jim, when can you come over? I want to see you."

"Tell you what—"

"When you talk like that, I know you're hiding something."

"Just as soon as I hear from Oona, I'll come over, all right? Incidentally, does everyone know? I mean have you told everybody?"

"Why? She didn't tell me not to."

"You have told everybody, then." He shook his head at the way she couldn't see, or refused to see, how her children could ever be at odds with one another. And in this one respect she was hopelessly mistaken—her children did not see eye to eye at all, and never would. In fact, what his mother didn't seem to realize was that if not for her the family would have broken apart long before this, and that when she died (God forbid) it would break apart, and with dispatch. It was her refusal to believe that her children were dissimilar in ideas, aspirations, political leanings and everything else, that made her, however unwittingly, such a troublemaker. He could just imagine the shock and indignation that Oona's "adoption" had already caused.

"Jim, *is* something wrong? Was I supposed to keep it a secret?"

"Ma, can't I ever ask you anything without your becoming suspicious?"

"If there's a letter from Oona in your box when you get home, then, you'll be here tomorrow."

"If. Now, Ma, I said I'd come over. I have to go now. I'll see you."

"All right, Jim. Come over, that's all. Because you know, and I know, you're not telling me the truth."

"Okay, Olga, I'll see you," he said, and thought, A good boot in the ass. If Oona were here now, I'd really give her one.

CHAPTER VI

70 *Morningside Drive*
New York 27, N.Y.
June 10, 1953

Dear Oona,

As per your letter to the family relating to an
adoption, please be advised that I am unalterably
opposed to any Italian orphan being given the
O'Hagen name. Accordingly, I wish to inform you
that, pursuant to your arrival from Italy, I will do
everything in my power to exempt Mama and Papa
from this—your latest whim.

Carrying my thoughts back to the days when I
was employed after high school every day by the
Atlantic and Pacific Tea Company, I recollect how
Mama, after the older girls got married, used to sit
for hours at the dining room table cutting out
Vogue patterns for you and Cathy, damaging her
eyes over dresses that even the private school children in the neighborhood couldn't afford. Later,
when I forsook college to lend a helping hand to
Papa, I acquainted Mama with my feelings on the
matter. I petitioned her to make you more responsible and self-reliant by sending you to the Singer

Sewing Machine School, but she did not comply with my wishes. I told her she was making an irremediable mistake, and various and sundry events have proven me right.

You abandoned Manhattanville College of the Sacred Heart and enrolled in that Communist New School for Social Research. I was hostile to that, I disfavored your living in the Village with those seven other lost and misguided girls, and I was militant against your going to Europe at all (what's wrong with America?), let alone unescorted. Now you no longer receive the sacraments of the Church, you believe in "freedom of the soul and body," and at twenty-four you are still without a husband.

I am fully cognizant of your affiliation with Jim, the other college graduate in the family, and your contempt for me. You have called me a "stuffed shirt" every Christmas now for the last ten years, and I have kept my countenance only in consideration of Mama and Papa, who are still gullible and naïve enough to be flattered and charmed by the nonsensical things you say to them, like calling Papa "the Ronald Colman of Riverside Drive."

But now, as I have always predicted, you have overextended yourself, and you are going to pay dearly for it. If I, as the steward of the family, the oldest son, and Papa's partner in the business, can help it, there will be no dark-skinned bambino in this neighborhood where the O'Hagen name is still

respected and where my four daughters live, worship
God, and go to Parochial School.

Yours truly,
KEVIN

Oona put the letter aside (the baby was asleep),
got a pad of paper from her desk drawer and
grabbed her pen as she might have a dagger. How
like Kevin to write such a letter. How like him,
mean by osmosis as well as design, to mail it so she
would receive it today, when things couldn't be
worse for her at the American Consulate and only a
few hours before her appointment there. As furious
and bitter as she had ever been in her life, she
couldn't write her reply fast enough.

June 18, 1953

Dear Kevin,

Your letter is amusing for "various and sundry"
reasons, but especially for the reason that you seem
to think everybody's memory is as faulty or distorted
as yours is. Don't you remember after the war, ex-
Chief Petty Officer Kevin, how you used to get all
dressed up in that homburg and form-fitting topcoat
of yours and go downtown, empty attache case and
all, looking for a job? I was only fifteen at the time,
but even then I wondered what happened inside

your pea bean of a soul when one interviewer after another saw through the pomposity, and with a handshake, a smile, and a "Don't call me, I'll call you," got rid of you. You "forsook" college not to help Papa with the business but to wheedle and coerce Papa (while Jim was "selfishly" getting his degree at Columbia) into making you a partner. Papa told me himself, several times, how you used to come by every day after your morning sortie with the employment agencies and tell him how to run the business. Fire one bartender and two waiters, you'd say, and stop believing customers when they say their steaks weren't done to perfection, etc.

You became a monkey on Papa's back, and Papa, too old or too soft to get you off, bought you the bar and grill for no other reason than to get rid of you. And do you remember how you criticized Papa for buying the place for you? It was painful to have to listen to you telling Mama what a stupid business man Papa was, how another bar and grill in the Wall Street area could not possibly succeed. But no sooner did Papa's simple menu idea prove him right, than you, "the steward of the family, the oldest son," wanted to be made a "legal" partner.

You know what I mean, Kevin? You're King of Kings in a drive-in theater with everybody in the car eating popcorn, and yet you think you're obligated to improve the manners and morals of everybody in New York with the possible exception of Cardinal

Spellman. As for what you said about my belief in
"freedom of the soul and body" . . .

Oona put her pen down to savor for a moment
the bitter pleasure of that incident. She and Kevin
were together by accident in the self-service elevator
at their parents' one day, and as was usually the case
when she was alone with him, her mind automatically started ticking off all the things that were
wrong with the world. There was nothing to say to
him, nothing she wanted to say, so when he pressed
the button and the elevator started upward, she did
her best to look as though she were listening to a
seashell held to her ear. It would have worked, too,
if it hadn't been Ash Wednesday and he hadn't
kept staring at her unsmudged forehead. His was so
generously thumbed with ash that Oona kept thinking, Could he have gone back for seconds? She
would have entertained no such thought about
anybody else, but irreverence seemed called for with
Kevin, and God, being God, would surely understand. It was indeed the fleeting conviction that
Kevin *had* gone back for seconds that had prompted
her to start listening to the seashell in the first place.
That is to say, she was not looking for trouble, but
his eyes (You haven't been for your ashes yet?)
wouldn't leave her forehead alone.

Finally, she turned to him and said, "Daughter

for a day. Would you like me to be your daughter
for a day?"

And just as she expected, he said, "You bet I
would."

"Tell me," she went on, "do you dominate your
children because you love them, or love them
because you dominate them?"

"I live up to the responsibilities of being their
father, if that's what you mean."

"That's not what I mean, but let it go." A
momentary silence, then—because the elevator was
probably the smallest and slowest in New York
City—she said, "Do you believe in freedom?"

"Of course I believe in freedom."

"Of the soul and body?"

If she had pulled Pontius Pilate out of her
handbag, Kevin could not have looked more
shocked. "Certainly not! Not that kind of freedom.
Do you?"

"Wait a minute, look at it this way," Oona said.
"You're here, in this elevator, and you think I'm
here with you. Right? But I'm not. I mean put that
in your pipe and smoke it."

Her face as she stared at him was as indeci-
pherable as a clock without hands. It was a trick she
used on Kevin because she knew he couldn't stand
having anyone escape with the loot, which to him
was anything he wanted that the other person had,
old newspapers even. Was she serious or wasn't she?

He didn't know, he wasn't sure, and the look on her face was giving him no help at all. She might have slipped behind the damask curtains her mother had made for the living room. Oona thought they were horrible, but they were thick at least.

"There's something wrong with you," Kevin said. "Something really wrong. There must be."

"You're wasting your time if you're talking to me. I'm simply not here."

"Now listen," he said, and she could see how much he wished she were his daughter for a day. "I've had enough!"

"But I tell you I'm at Bay Head. Over sixty miles from here. The thought of being alone in an elevator with you was too much. I had to leave."

No sooner did they get off the elevator and enter their parents' apartment than Kevin informed his mother of Oona's belief in freedom of the soul and body. Maggie O'Hagen, besides being incapable of thinking wrong of her daughters no matter what they did, had the sense of humor to put Kevin's accusation in its right perspective. But to placate her oldest son, she said, "Oona, will you please stop it? Every time you and Kevin are in the same room, this happens."

"But, Ma," Oona said, "why should I be his daughter for a day?"

"What do you mean, his daughter?" Maggie said, losing her sense of humor as Oona had known she would. "You're my daughter."

"Exactly!" Oona said. "And not even for a day do I want to be Kevin's."

Maggie O'Hagen was never funnier than when she tried to be the judicious matriarch. She turned with complete seriousness to Kevin and said, "You've got four daughters of your own."

"Ma, why do you let her do this to you all the time?" Kevin said.

"What has she done?" Maggie said. "Did you want her to be your daughter for a day, or not?"

"God is listening, Kevin," Oona said.

Everything became very confused after that, and the only thing Oona was sorry about afterward was the effect it probably had on Kevin's daughters when he got home. There were only four of them, and that night he desperately needed a fifth.

Oona picked up her pen to go on with her reply, but just thinking of that Ash Wednesday had taken the sting out of Kevin's letter. She reread what she had written with embarrassment, as she might have a page in an old diary—a page that would have to be ripped out if she was going to keep the diary. Kevin's opinion of her was as jaded as hers was of him. There was nothing to say, nothing she wanted to say—and what she had said would be unfair to her father.

She was tearing up her reply in little pieces, thinking, *Why such little pieces? I'm three thousand miles away,* when the maid came in from hanging clothes in the garden. How Maria knew a day would be sunny long before it became sunny (when it was still pretty dismal, in fact) mystified Oona, but without fail, if there were clothes soaking in the tub in the morning, it always turned out to be a sunny day. A talent like that fascinated Oona, probably because her mother had it too but had failed to pass it on to her. In fact she had often wondered, watching her mother putter about the house, why I.Q. tests never included items like, "Before answering the next set of questions, wet your finger and stick it out the window. Thirty second limit and only one wetting allowed." *She* had a pretty high I.Q., even if she said so herself, but when it came to things like that, her mother was *Einstein* compared to her.

"Signora, you will be late for the Consulate!" Maria said in the combination Italian and English they'd devised for communicating with each other. "Your dress, the white one with the eyes, your underwear, your stockings—everything is ready. Please, Signora, for the baby's sake, the passport, you must not be late."

Oona didn't know it at the time, but on the day the baby was born, every gardener and maid on the hill came over. Dr. Maderini allowed no one in but the five women who arrived with him, and they, being insiders by virtue of their having washed and dressed the baby, were asked all sorts of questions on the way back to town and in the town itself. Assuming Oona's name was Mrs. O'Hagen, they gave that name as the baby's surname to the commune in Fiesole: Sheila O'Hagen, daughter of Anthony and Oona O'Hagen. The "Anthony" was supplied by Maria, who had seen Tony at the villa every day during the first month of their stay, heard Oona call him Tony, cooked their meals and kept the fireplace going for them as she had during previous summers for other American couples. In fact, when Tony Friedensohn reneged and went back to his wife, Oona told Maria that he'd been called back to the States.

Several days later, when Oona found out about it from Dr. Maderini, she panicked. She unburdened herself to him, told him everything but the father's name, and asked him to go to the secretary of the commune and try to have the baby's Italian birth certificate changed to read: Sheila Penhaligan, daughter of Peter and Oona Penhaligan. She used "Peter Penhaligan" because she wanted her husband to be dead, and a man by that name, a friend, had died in New York shortly before her departure for Italy of a disease called lupus erythematosus. Oona had once seen a great deal of Peter Penhaligan, and having gone to his funeral and met his sister, she could, she thought, answer questions about him with more authority than she could about someone completely fictional. Then too, the disease, she thought, would lend more weight to her story than an ordinary coronary, since you didn't get a disease like lupus erythematosus out of a hat.

Dr. Maderini did as she asked and was told by the secretary of the commune, who must have suspected that the baby was born out of wedlock, that if she wanted to take the baby back to the United States with her, it would be better to leave the Italian birth certificate as it stood, since she at least (the mother) could definitely establish her American citizenship. Besides, he told Maderini, Oona might otherwise have trouble with the Italian authorities. So the certificate was sent to the American Consulate, where it was recorded that on May 13, 1953, an American woman, Oona O'Hagen, whose husband, Anthony O'Hagen, had been called back to the States, gave birth to a daughter.

Oona was furious, but then, realizing that she was going to have to have a story to tell her mother and father anyway, she decided to try to turn the thing to her advantage. If she were to adopt a baby in Italy (the story she finally did tell her mother and father and the one that provoked Kevin's letter) the baby's surname would be, or at least could be, the same as hers. This took care of her mother and father, but not the American Consulate, where she would naturally be asked who, what, and where, her husband was. Indeed, if Kevin's letter hadn't preceded by a matter of hours her appointment at the Consulate, if it hadn't unwittingly touched upon her real problem, of how she was going to get her baby back to America with her, it undoubtedly would not have made her so bitter.

After she had sponged off and fixed her hair and made up to conceal whatever pallor remained, she put on her white eyelet dress, the Leghorn hat she'd bought with Nancy at Ohrbach's Boutique Shop in New York, and Italian pumps as thin as spatulas.

Finally ready to go, she kissed Sheila very gently so as not to wake her, gave Maria instructions which she knew would not be heeded (even though Maria listened to them with great nods of approval and would have thought her remiss as a mother if she'd given no instructions at all), and left to take the "feeler" bus down to Florence. On the way a little blond boy got on and was measured against the conductor's meter stick (he was taller than the stick so he had to pay full fare) and Oona thought, will Sheila be paying full fare before this thing is settled?

After leaving the tram, more conscious than ever that she was going to the Consulate about her fictitious husband, she started over past Cathedral Square toward Friedensohn's office. She didn't expect to see him, but wanted to (or be seen by him, "the bastard"), if only because she'd had his daughter and lost her stomach and all.

It was one of those spring days that always beguiled her into thinking this *was* the best of all possible worlds, and to make matters worse, that is to say better, she happened to be walking through a part of Florence (cobblestone streets and "one-lane" sidewalks) that reminded her a little of old downtown New York. The buildings were two or three stories high and all dissimilar, and their many chimneys and slanting roofs even made the sky more interesting. Gardens with miniature black iron gates were fitted into "leftover" nooks and corners, and windows, even in the same house, were broad, narrow, tall, and sometimes even angular. There was very little to buy, but a well-displayed scarf or hat gave almost the opposite impression, which was fine, since she had no money to buy anything anyway.

Later, over near Cathedral Square, she passed a lank young American with a portable radio perched on his shoulder, and her response to seeing him, the suddenness of it after her lonely recuperation in the villa, was such an honest and wonderful thing in comparison to Kevin's letter that she slowed down just to prolong looking at him. He was wearing sun-glasses so his "whaddiyacallit"—personality, character, soul—was left out. He was simply her opposite, healthy and young, with red lips and white teeth, and she, feeling thin and beautiful

again, wanted just as simply to go up and kiss him.
Maybe eyes should always be that dark and round,
she thought as they passed each other, and the
whaddiyacallit that hidden. And maybe I should
stop *liking* men so much.

Then, just as she was going into one of her
favorite places for a quick cognac, she did see Tony.
He was walking at an angle away from her through
the square, and whether it was because he looked so
worried and sad, or because seeing him made her
feel that much more alone with the responsibility of
getting her daughter back to America, she recalled
that in New York, when she'd first become interested in him, she was glad he was Jewish because
she'd always wanted children and Jews made good
fathers. The recollection did not strike her as ironic.
She still thought Jews made better fathers than
Christians in general and Irish Catholics in particular. She excluded her father and brother Jim, but
not Kevin, for example, whose bigotries and pre-
conceptions seemed almost to have come into the
world with him, like stowaways from a former life.
True, an Irish father might be a great one for a
strong-willed child to react against, and that was to
the good if the child happened to be strong-willed.
If not, an Irish father could be disastrous in a way
that a Jewish father never was, slob though the
Jewish father might be about overfeeding his child,
overclothing him, and overexposing him to doctors,

dentists, and X-rays.

That Jewish father at her doctor's when she had gone for shots and a vaccination before leaving for Italy, for example. A real lulu. He had come in not as a patient but to see about his son, who had apparently just returned to Cornell after spring vacation and a series of chest X-rays. The doctor had a patient in the inner office and so brought the X-rays to the outer office where Oona was sitting, and from the very beginning, when the doctor adjusted a lampshade to get more light, it was obvious that X-rays were beyond the man—as mysterious-looking to him as they were to most laymen. This, however, did not deter or discourage the man—on the contrary, it made him that much more determined to know exactly what the X-rays meant. He was there to find out what they meant, and the more his eyes roamed over their foggy darknesses, the more Oona saw him as being out on a moor somewhere, in search of his son's soul. The doctor, Jewish himself, and perhaps for that reason very impatient with the man, kept telling him there was absolutely nothing wrong with his son's lungs, but the man couldn't help himself. He was out on this moor, and it wasn't the one in *Wuthering Heights*, it was his son's moor, the moor where his son did his breathing and all.

Finally, though, because she was next, she said in a very low whisper, almost to herself, "Calling

Scotland *Ya-ard!*" But she drew it out the way
Merle Oberon did in the picture when she called
Heathcliff, and the man heard her and didn't like it
at all. He was out on the moor, all right, he knew it
and she knew it, but he didn't want the Yard called
and a lot of bloodhounds sniffing around where his
son's innermost self was hidden. He wanted to do
all the sniffing himself.

Jewish fathers were slobs, she would be the first to
admit it, but Tony wasn't a slob, and she figured
that even if he were to become one, it would be nice
to know he loved the child she gave him. She didn't
want an orthodox Jew, no dogma or anything—just
a Jew, a cultured Jew, which was what she had got.
Leave it to her, though, to get the wrong one, a man
without a country in the truest sense of the phrase,
who held no malice toward anyone (because that
would upset the smooth operation of life), but who
had no stick-to-itiveness, and no real power to be
loyal either.

What struck her most, though, was that Tony
had existed right up to this moment of her seeing
him in the Piazza del Duomo, and now already she
was thinking, Florence was so different with Tony
here. He wasn't out of sight and she was thinking
that. She didn't understand it.

At the American Consulate, she found herself at
a desk across from a Mr. Johnson, who kept asking
her questions and filling in a form called Report of

Birth Abroad of a Citizen of the United States. Oona had no way of knowing it at the time (she could have found out, and would have, if in New York she had been more circumspect in her dealings with Tony), but for a person born outside the United States of American parents, this form, also called a Consular Report of Birth, was the very basis of that person's claim to United States citizenship. The trouble in Oona's case was that it had to be approved before they would give her a Certification of Birth (which she needed to get the baby's passport), and there she was swearing that her husband's name was Anthony O'Hagen and that he was at present in the United States.

The vice-consul, Mr. Johnson, and two other men were there, and they not only seemed to know all about the birth (the name of the milk woman who went for Dr. Maderini, the name of Oona's maid, etc.), they gave her the feeling that they were proud of her. In any event they were extremely kind and even invited her to their Fourth of July tea, or cocktail party, Oona never became certain which. Perhaps if they hadn't been so friendly, she would have been more on guard against what came next, which she was sure was not a trap—she just didn't expect it.

Mr. Johnson had filled in the form and given it to the vice-consul, who had begun to drift over with it, half in and half out of the conversation, to another desk. Oona and the others went on talking and it was all very casual and nice except for one thing. They kept sympathizing with her about her husband's absence when she knew perfectly well that he didn't exist. "You say he's in New York?" they asked. "Does he know?" "Have you heard from him?" "How proud he's going to be when he hears what you've done. How proud we are," etc., until she got a little tired of it.

Just then, when she was most tired of it, the vice-consul called over, "Mrs. O'Hagen, when do you expect him?"

"What was that? I'm sorry," she said to the vice-consul.

"Mr. O'Hagen. When do you expect him?"

In a desperate attempt to avoid further questions about her husband (let him answer the questions, she thought, with a resentment she was sure she would never have felt toward Peter Penhaligan), she blurted out, "Very shortly."

"Oh, well, in that case," the vice-consul said, "we'll just leave this pending until he arrives."

Oona walked over to him, laughing to hide her nervousness. "But when he does arrive, he's going to be—I mean, he hasn't even seen the baby yet. Couldn't I get this settled now? Isn't my passport enough?"

"Mrs. O'Hagen, I understand perfectly how you feel. And I certainly don't want you to think we're here to make things difficult for you. We're here to help you." He gave her what she later came to think of as his smile of smiles. "We don't sponsor art shows for Americans over here, or make hotel reservations, or endorse new religious sects, but we *can* be of help if a problem comes under our jurisdiction. Here"—he got something from a drawer—"let me show you why your passport isn't enough. This is a copy of our Immigration and Nationality Act of 1952. Now, since you and your husband are both citizens of the United States, the Consular Report of Birth, which is this form here, the form Mr. Johnson was just filling out for you, must be approved under the provisions of Section 301, Subsection (a) Item (3) of the Immigration and Nationality Act. And under these provisions, positive proof of the United States citizenship of both parents is required." He gave her that smile again, his smile of smiles. "It's as simple as that."

"Well, I don't want you to break the law, or anything like that," Oona said. "My husband will come by with his passport, then."

"Goodness, Mrs. O'Hagen. It'll only take a minute, and the Consular Report of Birth is very important. Once it's approved, a copy of it goes to our State Department in Washington, where it's kept permanently on file as proof of your daughter's citizenship. All Americans born outside the United States are protected in the same way." He handed

her the copy of the Immigration and Nationality
Act. "Why don't you take this along with you? And
meanwhile, please don't forget our Fourth-of-July
party."

This was what she always left out of account—the
part accident played in her life. If her maid hadn't
told the commune in Fiesole that her husband's
name was "Anthony O'Hagen" and that before
leaving for the United States he'd lived at the villa
and eaten all his meals there, she could have had a
dead husband like Peter Penhaligan. Or, if that
wouldn't have worked, she could have "bought" an
Italian marriage certificate (Dr. Maderini's original
suggestion) and said she was married to an alien, in
which case her daughter would have been held to be
a United States citizen at birth if only because she
was a citizen.

Even now, if she went back to the Consulate and
told the truth, that her daughter was born out of
wedlock, Sheila would still, automatically, being her
daughter, be held to be a United States citizen. But
then the Consular Report of Birth would have to
say Sheila was born out of wedlock, and Oona did
not want information of that kind on file in the
State Department in Washington. What if Sheila
became an actress or a candidate for Congress or
something? She could just see the newspaper head-
lines thirty or forty years from now: "Candidate for
Congress Born Out of Wedlock."

If only she had had extra-long Fallopian tubes or something; she might have gone on merely wanting to have a baby. Now her daughter couldn't leave the country without a passport, and she couldn't go back for it without explaining why her husband didn't arrive, why she couldn't have her marriage certificate sent over from America, and all the rest of it. She had not planned to go to the Fourth-of-July party (the Consulate was a long walk from the tram stop and she couldn't afford a taxi), but now she would have to if only to stay on the good side of the vice-consul and lay the ground-work for some plan. If there had been something wrong with Sheila, if she had had some little defect—all right, Mrs. Friedensohn might not have been so anxious to become the child's legal mother. But a beautiful girl, Tony's own daughter—"perfection," the five Italian women had said, "with long blonde hair, long fingers, and a high, noble brow." What better balm for that woman's foot problem?

There was not a moment to lose. She must talk to Dr. Maderini and he usually came to the villa at this time. She had no one else *to* talk to, and yet if she couldn't trust him, if she knew that little about people, she'd better go back and ask her mother and father for *their* marriage certificate.

High heels hitting hard against the pavement, she hurried back to the Piazza San Marco and boarded a parked Fiesole trolley. Would he be there, enormously so despite the thin black worsted suit he always wore? Would he be sitting in the chair by the window or walking back and forth in the garden with that wonderful look of pain on his face? Not that walking pained him. What it did, apparently, was trigger something in his mind that showed as pain on his face. There goes a man who really thinks life's a struggle, Oona would have said if she were passing him, a stranger, in the street. But he didn't think that at all. Even when he was walking he didn't think it. He just became captain of the ship when he was on his feet, that was all, and Oona knew how captains were, how they were always telegraphing orders to the engine room, ordering "hard rights" and "hard lefts" and all that. In fact, she couldn't go for a walk with him without becoming convinced, just from glancing at him, that he really was up there on the bridge bringing the ship with its machinery, cargo, equipment and crew safely and expeditiously to port so the voyage would be as profitable as possible to the owner.

She had never spoken to him about it because it was one of those special things about a person that you wouldn't change for anything in the world. If he were really in pain—of course not. She wouldn't walk with him. But he loved to walk and was always asking her to go walking with him. He just couldn't walk any other way, that was all.

Another wonderful thing about him was that if

he had any preconceived ideas about how a young lady should act, he didn't want her to live up to them. Just yesterday, for example, he had said he didn't see how she could make a habit of doing what he least expected her to do. She smiled. Because wasn't that nice of him? He wanted her to surprise and delight and even shock him, in other words, and when she did, she forgot about Tony Friedensohn and felt all kinds of erratic desires for renewal. Even her familiarity with the villa came as a surprise; she saw the floor, the chair, the table in the kitchen where she read, and loved it all again. Maderini liked her, that was why, not what she was supposed to be or might someday become. He liked her as she was, and right now that was what she needed. Oh, how she needed that, how she needed him, right now.

CHAPTER VII

Dr. Maderini had come and gone, Maria said, and when Oona heard that, she just sat there, thinking of Theodore Dreiser. It took guts, Dreiser's kind of guts, to make life this repetitiously disappointing. Like that time in Chicago—Oona remembered it so well—when Sister Carrie went looking for a job. Did Dreiser get her one right away? No sir. Not Dreiser. He practically turned his back on her during that whole section of the book. If Carrie wanted a job, let her go out and get one. No favors from Theodore Dreiser. No letters of introduction. No rich uncle dropping out of one of the elm trees on Main Street. It was sad in a way, because you could tell he really liked Sister Carrie. He wasn't refusing her the letters of introduction to be cruel or anything like that. He just didn't believe in recommending inexperienced girls for jobs, that was all.

Oona stood up. She felt worse than the night she had returned to the villa and found no wood for the fire. Was Dreiser right? Did victory have to come this hard? Even a little victory like Maderini's being here?

*   *   *

If I sound bitter [she went on to Jim and Nancy, for she had to talk, or write, to somebody], it's because yesterday, before Kevin's letter even arrived, I was seriously thinking of using a razor on myself and Sheila. There was no baby food at all, only bread, in the house. I took some clothes, those three gray rugs McManus sent to me by mistake, my engagement ring, and the express ticket for my radio in Genoa, and sold them to a dealer in Florence for about one-fourth their value ($300). I've paid bills, bought things for the baby, and will be very careful with what's left.

I realize now, though, that I cannot afford to rent an apartment in New York, pay some woman to mind the baby while I work, and buy the woman's, the baby's, and my food unless I make $200 a week, which is almost twice my usual salary. If the baby and I are not allowed to live at home with Mama and Papa at least for a while, I don't see how I can go home. I'm not going to wander around New York *looking* for a place to stay, and yet I have to go somewhere, since the rent here is paid only through the month of September. I'd like to know what Mama and Papa think, how *they* feel about it, and what I can't understand is why *they* don't write. I've written them four or five letters on this one subject alone, but only Cathy (their Boswell) writes me. I know Mama's eyes are bad, but she could dictate to Cathy, and if that's what she does do, then Cathy doesn't know how to take dictation.

In a letter I received in the same mail with Kevin's, for example, Cathy starts off by saying that *she's* surprised at how well Mama and Papa took the news about the baby. They suspect Sheila's mine, she said, but have said nothing outright. I should say Sheila's mine if she is, she said, because if it were to make a difference, the difference would be in my favor; they would be that much more anxious to see her.

Cathy's no Kevin, so don't misunderstand me, but then she goes on to say that it would be "impossible" for the baby and me to live at home, that Mama and Papa are "too old" to have an infant under their feet. Mama and Papa may be old, but if any two people in this world are in the stream of life, they are. Infants therefore *belong* under their feet. Besides, are they that much older all of a sudden? I've only been *gone* a few months.

Then she says that I should get an apartment, that "my friends" could start now to look for one for me, and that with the money I'd make myself, and the money I'd "receive" for the baby every month (Where did she get that idea? She's going places, that girl), I'd make out "beautifully." She mentions in passing the additional problem of "space"—for a bathinette, a crib, a playpen, etc. She's crazy. Sheila sleeps with me, gets a little sponge-off on the kitchen table, and has never seen a playpen, let alone the inside of one. Sheila's out all day in the garden with me and at home she'd be out in the park in a carriage.

Papa still sleeps in the "maid's" room off the kitchen, doesn't he? Well, if I were to get my king-size bed out of Lincoln and have it put in Mama's room in place of her three-quarter bed, why couldn't Mama, Sheila, and I sleep together? Sheila would not "wake Mama at five or six o'clock every morning," as Cathy says. She wakes up at eight or nine and never cries—just pulls my hair or kicks me.

She forgets that there was a time when she and I and Mama and Papa and you, Jim, all lived in that same apartment. But I know what she means, because the apartment actually grew smaller after you moved into the Columbia dorms and left. Cathy began closing the door to the back bedroom and I began filling the emptied bookshelves with my books. A year later, when I started living in the Village, the apartment must have grown still smaller. Cathy must have consolidated certain gains, been glad to see me go. That's the way it is, and I don't blame her.

She's putting up obstacles, I think, to hide the fact that Kevin and his bambino phobia are having an effect on Mama and Papa. I'm therefore taking her advice and admitting to Mama and Papa, in a letter I'll be mailing with this one, that the baby *is* mine. I'll tell them the truth except for one detail. I'll say I was secretly married last September in Maryland to a man named Peter Penhaligan, who's dead. He really is—I went to his funeral. Anyway, they know I was in Maryland in September, so the date will "fit." And I like the sound of Sheila Penhaligan, don't you?

While Mama and Papa are coming to a decision, I'll be trying to get the baby's birth report and passport from the Consulate. I have to act within the next three weeks for two reasons. One, the vice-consul, who said he'd wait for my husband to arrive, is on vacation. Two, Dr. Maderini, who says he'll accompany me to the Consulate as a good friend of my husband's, is leaving for some sort of medical meeting in Rome next month.

If you would help me, Jim, I'd like to go back to the Consulate with a letter from you explaining why my husband didn't, and cannot, join me in Europe as planned. I'd write the letter and send it to you (and I know what to say), if you'd copy and send it back to me. Would you, Jim? Dr. Maderini will accompany me to the Consulate but will say nothing about knowing my husband unless called upon to do so. I think the letter, with its U.S. postmark, will be sufficient. If it isn't (even with Maderini's help), I'll just have to get the Consular Report approved under the born-out-of-wedlock section of our Immigration and Nationality Act. At least *I'm* an

American citizen, and thank God I can prove it.

Meanwhile, since I cannot afford to go on storing furniture that I may never use, I wonder if you would mind trying to sell it for me. Lincoln handles the whole thing (my former boss had them sell some stuff for him), so you would just have to be there to authorize the sale. Not counting what's in the cartons, the furniture is valued by Lincoln at $3,100, so you should get $1,000 anyway. The dining room chairs are still in their excelsior wrappings, the bedroom furniture is virtually untouched; the bureaus and chests have never been used, etc. I know the dining room table has a liquor stain, but it could be lacquered. As for the pictures, records, ironing board, dishes, shower curtains, hamper, bread box, garbage pail, and so forth, I would just as soon keep them since they usually, in such a sale, go for nothing.

If Mama and Papa say I can stay with them for a while, I'll be able to leave (assuming the Consulate gives me a passport for the baby) just as soon as you send me the money. If Mama and Papa say I cannot stay with them, I'll need the money just to go on living here. Never again do I want to feel as I did yesterday, when I actually went to the medicine chest to see if I had an unused razor blade (though why it had to be unused I don't know). I just can't *stand* it when there's no food for the baby, and no one in all Italy to ask for help but Tony Frieden-

sohn, the one person in the world I refuse to ask. I
know I've exhausted my credit with you, but I think
Lincoln even puts its own ad in the paper, for both
sales and auctions. You can find out by telephoning.

Wait. I just thought of something and think I'll
try it on the chance that you can't sell the furniture
or are offered about three dollars for it. The Magnavox, the one item under the name of Friedensohn
(Tony got it for me for my birthday), was bought at
Altman's for $600. It has never even been plugged
in. The wires are still coiled, the tags are on,
cardboard protectors are still around the dials, etc.

I'm writing the store manager, asking for a refund
on the grounds that, being forced to leave for
Europe the day it arrived, I could not arrange to
have it returned. I'm also telling him that it has
never been used, that it is now at Lincoln, and that
you have access to the storeroom and the authority
to have it removed.

Even if he agrees to a partial refund, I'll be in four
or five hundred dollars which will be more than
enough to get me home if Mama and Papa say
yes.

What do you think? I'm giving the manager your
name, address, and telephone number, so if you
hear from him and he agrees to a refund, even to a
$300 refund, don't quibble with him.

Oh! About the stuff that I said I'd like to keep.
Could it be stored in your apartment-house base-

ment? Is there a storeroom? If not, have you any suggestions?

Please write. I need your letters now more than ever.

Love,
Oona O'

She put the letter with her outgoing mail and sat thinking, rocking back and forth, in "Maderini's chair." Until things sorted themselves out, should she try to get a job in Florence—at "Macy's," Cookes or some other American firm—and stay in Italy until Sheila was five or six months old? How were salaries in New York? Were jobs still easy to find? Just last week she'd received a letter from a man who'd lost his job at the photographer's studio where she'd worked before leaving for Italy. According to him New York was hysterical and unemployment increasing all the time, but she didn't believe him because aside from his political leanings (he called himself a middle-of-the-road communist), he was sixty-four and slowly going blind, and eyesight was essential to his work as a retoucher.

Really, she didn't know what to do, and meanwhile she was always going back in her mind to the old Morningside Heights neighborhood where she was born—to the stores, the people, and certain trees and benches in the park. Money would of

course solve all but her American Consulate problems, and perhaps even those. Money! She would
never have believed that the lack of it could give
such a mean twist to things. She was always watching herself now—no, first came a feeling of dis-
comfort, interference, of something blocking her
happiness for a moment. I should be enjoying this,
she'd say to herself, but I'm not. Then she'd force
her mind past a barrier, the very barrier behind
which lay whatever was preventing her from enjoying herself. And in that way she usually found
out what it was. Someone had said something, she'd
done or not done something. It might be pride,
self-criticism, envy, hate, fear—any number of
things. But it was usually better to know.

The maid and baby were asleep. Siesta, the
loneliest time of the day if you were lonely. She got
up and went to the baby, little Sheila, and lay in bed
next to her. Then with Sheila's unbelievably delight-
ful smell in her nostrils—a little victory easily won—
she went to sleep herself.

CHAPTER VIII

Dr. Maderini, same black worsted suit, same bulk, same painful-looking walk, came the next day about three hours after Oona had put on a huge kettle of her oxtail soup. Though obviously seized by the smell, he offered no comment as Oona, familiar with the ways of his visits, kicked off her pumps and stepped onto the scale (an old-fashioned but very accurate one he had lent her for the duration of her stay at the villa) for her weigh-in.

"Thank you for waiting yesterday, Elio," she said, arms folded, eyes (with the help of the scale) on a level with his. "You knew I was going to the Consulate. You knew I'd want to talk to you about it. You knew I'd have no one else to talk to."

"Oona, you are moving. No, you are jumping. Stop, please."

He slid the heavier of the two weights along the upper bar to the niche marked fifty kilograms. Too much. Back to forty-five kilos. Still too much. She has lost weight, then. Back to forty-four kilos, then the smaller weight along the lower bar to ten, fifteen, twenty-two, thirty grams.

"Oona, in two days . . . look at me, Oona. Please listen to me. In two days you have lost almost a kilo."

"After yesterday—what'd you expect?" She stepped down from the scale and back into her pumps. "What did you say a kilo was again?"

"More than two pounds. You have lost almost a kilo—about two pounds."

"All together, in pounds, what do I weigh?"

"Less than one hundred pounds. Let us say ninety-seven pounds. You are too tall, Oona, a meter and sixty-seven centimeters—"

"Five feet, six inches, Elio. You promised."

"Still, the weight is not enough." He went to his bag for his diagnostic tools. "You have a urine specimen for me?"

"Before you leave. I forgot this morning." She extended her arm for the application of the blood-pressure strap and was momentarily silenced, touched, by how kindly his eyes passed over the pale, faintly veined skin of her underarm. Her loss of weight had disappointed him; she had disappointed him. And she couldn't have that. "Look at how small my wrists are," she said to anger him a little. "Don't you feel sorry for me?"

He took her blood pressure and pulse and wrote out three prescriptions, for pills, a tonic, cough medicine. Oona put them on her desk with her outgoing mail, but knew she would never—could not afford to—have them filled. The deceit, though, or the pride behind it, turned her into herself. She became depressed, and she could look more depressed while she was depressed (though she was never depressed for long) than someone, say, in an asylum who was a real pro at it.

Maderini, giving her some of her own back, said, "Where is that charming young girl who was just here? Did you see her go?" For though he knew immediately when something was wrong, he always associated it with what he called the "discontinuity of Americans," never with the lack of money of Americans. Oona was not going to straighten him out because she much preferred being discontinuous than poor. Who wouldn't? And yet if she had had money somewhere, anywhere, even hidden in some shack in the flats of New Jersey, she would not have hesitated to ask him for the prescriptions on credit. Nor would she have lost anything by asking him, since money even made you sexy. Not money in your pocketbook; money in your head.

Maderini, his tools back in his bag, was walking back and forth, telegraphing orders to the engine room again, ordering hard rights and hard lefts and all the rest of it. When it became obvious that the smell of her oxtail soup had really piqued his curiosity (the caraway seeds had him fooled), she let him suffer a little longer. Then she began to suffer, for it was her soup, damn it, and she could

tell he had reached the point where he felt chal-
lenged by the smell. If curiosity were a color and he
were painted with it, he would die now before he
would admit he was curious. Were all Italians this
obvious and childlike? Why didn't he get down on
his knees and sniff?

"All right, Elio, stop! That's enough! Either go to
the kitchen and *see* what it is, or admit you've been
beaten."

"You saw my interest?"

"Didn't you see me fall through the floor? How
could I have?"

"Oona, with us, why is it always one question and
then another question? What about answers? We
have four questions now and no answers."

"How could I help seeing your interest? Is that
what you mean?"

"Six questions. Good. Let us pile them up. The
maid has prepared something new?"

"Never mind. Would you like some?"

"Why don't you admit it? The maid has prepared
something new?"

"Why don't *you* admit you've been beaten?"

He smiled. Between them they had made up a
dozen unanswered questions. Still, she also was at
fault. They were both at fault. Every day, in the
beginning when he came, they must bicker like this.
They must pretend no pleasure to hide the pleasure.
All right, she was alone all day, and the baby could

not talk to her. She became stretched tight. But who did she think she was fooling?

"I promise, Oona. You answer me—I answer you." Really, he would not be her friend if he did not annoy her just a little more. "The maid has prepared something new?"

"No! This is *my* dish. Maria didn't touch a carrot of it."

"Ah, *that* is why all the questions. You are—" He hesitated as if straining for a phrase. He wasn't, but he wanted something out of this too, and her face—he loved to watch it take on assignments for him, loved to test its capacity and see if there were things it couldn't do. Even counting the faces of children, he had never seen one so ready and eager to go places with him, or *for* him, it didn't matter which. That elusive phrase, for example. He could stop straining for it now. Her face was doing all that for him. But enough. Her face needed a rest. "All the same," he went on, "I will have some. Delighted! I must see if the smell and the taste—I must compare them and see."

"You're staying, then, Elio, for lunch. Go to the garden and I'll call you. The baby's there with Maria so you can examine her while you're waiting."

What would she have done if he'd had to leave immediately to see another patient? But he was still in the room with her, still looking at her, only now, suddenly, his face was sad. It was a way he had, suddenly looking sad for no reason. She didn't understand it. "You're *supposed* to look at the baby when you come, Elio."

"You. I am here to look at you. Not the baby. You are the sick one. Not the baby."

After he had gone, she got out the tablecloth and napkins she had brought over from her Irving Place apartment in New York (never used, the Bloomingdale sticker still on them), and prepared for their first lunch together, the first bit of food for him she had ever made. Thrilled, and nervous too, she kept asking herself, *Why*, for goodness sake? She just liked the guy, that was all. And he liked her. God, he was at least a thousand years old. He didn't look it, though. He looked a lot younger than that, in fact.

Ordinarily she ate here and there at the villa, at this or that table, depending on her mood or the time of day. Now it was sunny and warm and he would be dining with her, so she set the table by the window with the view: hills of green wheat and wildflowers reaching down to an old retaining wall, beyond which, for miles, stretched the Arno Valley below. She could see the buildings and palaces of Florence doing what Maderini called "their geometry homework in the sun." And yet the villa had become a golden prison, for she had few visitors now and rarely went down to Florence any more.

Maderini still came, but even his visits, prized by her though they were, made her think of money the moment they were over. How would she ever pay him? On the very day the baby was born, before the five Italian women had even left, she had asked him what his fee would be. And what had he done? Thrown his palms up as though she had handed him a hot poker. What a thing to do to him, hand him anything that hot! But what about his fee, damn it? Did he think she was wealthy? What a shock he was in for if he did.

The table set, some cheese in a plate, a fresh, seeded loaf of bread in a basket, a bottle of table wine uncorked and ready, she went to the kitchen to see about the soup. Maderini didn't know it, but she had made the soup, gallons of it, because once it cooled, if you heated only what you needed each day, it could easily last you a week. You really didn't need anything else, not even bread, because everything was in it—meat, bone marrow, herbs, and just about every vegetable in existence.

When she removed the cover, the meat and tomato colors were dominant, but the other colors weren't fooling anybody, they were there too. Like when she was a child and she got a box of crayons. As a starter she would rub all the colors in the same place on a piece of paper, really mix and tangle them until their legs became so crazy and entwined that they would leave off even having legs and

become one of the stained-glass windows at Corpus
Christi Church.

She got a tablespoon and sort of freed the steam-
ing surface of the soup of everything special—
molecules of fat and meandering streaks of other
light stuff—and then dipped in for about half a
spoon of the real thing, the soup itself. She blew on
it and waited, looking down at the spoon, lips
puckered. Don't burn your tongue. Ma never did.
Patience. The young girls nowadays don't have it.
They'll learn, though, won't they, Ma? The hard
way. . . . Her eyes wrinkled with amusement as a
daydream formed just over the spoon's horizon. By
the way, Ma, how come no one's ever seen your
marriage certificate? Where is it? The back-bedroom
closet, eh? Is that why no one's ever seen it? Why
no one's probably ever going to see it? What a place
to put something like that, in with everybody's
winter clothes, all the Christmas-tree things, Cathy's
Flexible Flyer, my jodhpurs and boots, dress and
curtain material, old lamps, the shillelagh Pa used
when he was a runner for Tammany, and God
knows what else! (The shillelagh she would throw
in for color, and to hear her mother's denials: What
shillelagh? Your father never owned one. He never
ran for Tammany or anyone else.)

I promise not to mention the shillelagh again,
then, Ma. Unless we come across it while we're
looking for the certificate. I won't even mention it if

we do come across it. I don't care about the
shillelagh, it's the certificate I'm interested in. I
mean you say you're legally married to Papa, right?
Everybody in the neighborhood thinks you're legally
married to Papa. Your children, at least the ones
I've spoken to about it, think you're legally married
to Papa. But *are* you legally married to Papa? So
let's hop to. I'll work on the high stuff, those heavy
cartons you always tie with cake-box string, and you
take the trunk and suitcases on the bottom . . .

She tasted the soup. Marvelous. Best she'd ever
made. But would *he* like it? He didn't get that huge
body of his from going on fasts. He must really
know food. The smell and the taste, he'd said. I
must compare them, to see. To see what? Whether
she should be shot at dawn?

Cover back on and light off, she went to the
garden where little Sheila and Maderini—not a word
—were having a combination eye-fight and chinning
match. Sheila, almost mesmerized, had hold of
Maderini's two forefingers and was making a chinning bar of them. She kept straining to pull herself
up, her face red, her mouth awry, then suddenly let
go and smiled. A victorious smile it was, though,
nothing uncertain or defeated about it. She had
beaten Maderini on both counts, she thought. She
was a born winner, that Sheila was. Just wait'll
Theodore Dreiser got a hold of her.

"She sees me," Maderini said. "She knows me. I am sure of it."

More herself now that Maderini had been with her awhile, Oona said with that ring of sincerity to which he always so quickly responded, "Sometimes I see the most wonderful look of concern and concentration in her eyes. As though she were trying to arrange the sheet folds around her head in a combination that will last forever. Do *all* infants do that, or do you suppose she does it because she almost didn't get into the world?"

"She is amazed, Oona. All infants are amazed. That is to say, she is in the world at last. And the world amazes her. That is what you see, her amazement." Like a weary priest giving benediction to the scrubwomen at the six o'clock Mass, he did something vague and unemphatic with his right hand. "If only we didn't lose that. The amazement."

"Elio, what's the matter? Is something making you sad?"

"Questions again. Now we have two."

Suddenly, because she wanted him to be happy, not sad, she grabbed him with both hands around the throat. "Maderini, I mean it!"

Maria, off to one side, knew her too well to be alarmed. She half turned away even, to giggle. The old man, Oona was making him crazy too.

"Elio, listen!" Oona whispered when she saw

Maria giggling. "Cry for help. Come on, mean it."

Maderini made her very proud of him at that moment. He didn't cry, he gasped for help. Actors' Studio? Who needed one in Italy?

Maria turned, concerned, frightened, terrified. Oona's face, if it was not truly the face of a strangler—"Oona, no!" She rushed over, hands outstretched to stop the senseless murder. "Don't."

"No, I have changed my mind. Let her," Maderini said. He even waved goodbye to Maria and said, "Remember me."

Maria looked almost bashful as she broke down and laughed, but even so, she could not resist giving the doctor a piece of her mind. Oona could be crazy. Oona was crazy. But did he have to be crazy? She was not a doctor. He was. And so on.

Whereupon Maderini, duly contrite, followed Oona into the villa for lunch. The amazement, though—he should not have said it. He must be more careful. He had wanted her to know (without really knowing) that no matter how long she lived —but did he know how long she would live? Was he sure? With Oona could anyone ever be sure? In America they had everything new. She could live until she was fifty-five, maybe even sixty. Besides, what good to be sad? She was right. Also, she was smart. He must stop looking at her that way!

When Oona came in with the tureen of soup, she

was almost sorry she had invited him. It was only oxtail soup, and yet there he was, all napkin from his chin downward, and looking so massive, round and serious that it was as if she were going before a gourmet tribunal. After she had served him (No, thank you, she'd wait until King Tut told her what he thought of it), he sat in absolute silence, sipping spoon after spoon of it with that expression she had sometimes seen on solitary diners in good restaurants. That rotund little gourmet she had watched at Le Valois in New York one day, for example—he had had the same expression. It was an inward-looking expression full of such sensuous undertones that if, say, the gourmet had seen her looking at him, they both would have been embarrassed. It was that kind of expression, and for the gourmet that kind of experience. While she was sitting there at Le Valois, in fact, a friend of the gourmet's, a brisk Bulldog Drummond type with a homburg and mustache, came in and asked the gourmet if he could join him. The answer was of course yes, but from then on disenchantment set in. The gourmet went on eating, but except for little fugitive joys here and there, when his taste buds caught him unawares, he acted as though he and the food were breaking the law right there in front of his friend.

Maderini was that gourmet exactly, except for one tremendous difference—he wasn't in the least self-conscious. He carried on the same kind of discourse with every morsel he put in his mouth, only he could have been on television "live" and it wouldn't have made the slightest difference.

After he had had about ten spoons without uttering a word, she couldn't stand it any more. "What are you," she said, "a sadist?"

He came up from the depths of himself and smiled. "What do you mean?"

"You're not performing an autopsy! It's soup, for goodness sake. Soup! That's all."

"I am trying very hard to be sure."

"Of what?"

"I do not know 'of what.' You Americans! A person can want to be sure without knowing 'of what.' That is to say, a person can want to be sure of something so indefinite to begin with, that even when he *is* sure, he is not very sure what he is sure of."

"All right, *are* you sure?"

"Yes, I am very sure," he said, and that was all. He went back to sipping the soup again.

Oona sat there watching him (and she could almost see the protein blocks building up within his body), but he went right on sipping the soup as though he were absolutely alone in a hut somewhere.

"Do you like it?" she said, bending way over so that her head was on a level with the bowl.

"But, my dear, of course I like it. You are an

excellent cook. Also, you have put yourself into this soup. That is why I like it." He gave her that smile again, and suddenly she knew he had been pulling her leg all the time.

"Now your turn," he said. "You have some."

"I'll have some. Don't worry about it."

"I am not worried. I just want you to join me. Will you?"

"I don't feel like it now. Besides, I'd rather watch you."

"Oona, please. I must have the urine."

"Why, you—so that's it. You didn't stay for lunch because of the soup or to spend a little extra time with me. You just didn't want to go away empty-handed. As far as you're concerned, the only interesting thing about me is my urine. Everything else I can keep, is that it? Just give you the urine and you'll go."

"Not true, Oona. You know that is not true. Your urine, yes. I admit"—he raised his left hand, thumb and forefinger together, as if to soften the violins ever so slightly—"it interests me."

"The way you say that, Elio. The way you look when you say it. I could have you locked up, do you know that?"

"A doctor cannot be interested?"

"Not that way he can't."

" 'Way.' What means 'way'?"

"Easy. Let's say there are two adjoining rooms.

One is a small, neat, well-lighted laboratory with a long worktable, Bunsen burners, test-tube racks, chemicals in jars, instruments, a metal sink and so on. All right? And the other room is very large and kind of round, with a rotundalike ceiling, very thick Chinese silk rugs, satin-covered walls, dim amber lamps, feathery sofas and chairs, candelabras and all kinds of leather inlay work all around. The kind of room that turns sunlight into wine, and conversations into murmurous things that you just know would be interesting as hell if you could only hear them."

"Enough. I see clearly the two rooms."

"You not only see them, Maderini. You've got my urine specimen in the wrong room!"

What to do with her? Never before, not in forty years of medicine, had he known such a treacherous and wily patient to treat. Ten minutes with her and he began to doubt the validity of his diagnosis. Half an hour with her and he was ready to discard the diagnosis and start all over. An hour with her and he wanted to apologize for having thought she was sick. And it would always be so, always, no matter how sick she became, for she took only her healthy side into her confidence, allowed only her healthy side to whisper plots and strategems in her ear—anything to outwit, confuse or circumvent him, her own doctor! Other patients—once, twice, perhaps three times in their lives—saw the absurdity at the heart of tragedy. But Oona, she lived there, right where tragedy became absurdity. It was her permanent address. So what to do? Tell her she was absurd? Or tell her she was tragic? Or should he be sad? But why be sad? It was her place, wasn't it? All right, let her have it. She deserved it. All the same, he had no business treating her. Perhaps another doctor, one who had never heard of that address and would not believe it even existed, would be able to help her. But such a doctor, even if he were able to convince her she was sick, would such a doctor be the one to make her well? Make her want to get well? So it was a circle, really. What to do with her? He did not know.

"Oona, on my word. The other thing can wait. You can send Maria over with it later. Now I want to enjoy this soup. With you I want to enjoy it."

She relented, served him more and then served herself some, while he cut more bread.

"Bread?"

"Yes, thank you."

"Cheese?"

"Yes, thank you."

"Wine?"

"I thought you said I shouldn't."

"A little. With the soup."

They ate without speaking, without even looking at each other. Only sounds passed between them.

Good sounds, though, Oona thought, tame little sounds that you could take or leave. Like goldfish almost. Nice to have around. None of that polly-want-a-cracker stuff. If only, though, the soup would hurry up and become that damn urine he wanted, she might enjoy the next bowl . . .

Wait. Don't say anything. He's sad again. With food in his mouth this time, and if there's anything sadder than that, it's crying with food in your mouth. Was it Papa who cried with the mashed potatoes in his mouth that time? Or Jim? But anyway—

"Elio, listen, I'm sorry if I said anything to hurt your feelings."

"You did not. You never do, Oona. I am waiting, that is all. You said the Consulate, and so far, nothing. So I am waiting, wondering why nothing about the Consulate."

So, while he served her soup, bowl after bowl of it, she told him what had happened at the Consulate. Looking at her, he did not see how she could have room for so much soup, but he didn't know Oona when it came to oxtail soup. They talked and talked and made plans for her next assault on the Consulate, and Maderini even got his urine specimen before he left. Oona, walking him to his car, handed him the jar wrapped in brown paper.

"No," he said. "Really?"

"Be nicer to me, Elio. Much nicer, you hear? Or I

may start rationing it."

"No, Oona, please. Do not ration it." He started the motor and shifted into first, but held the clutch down. "What pleasure for me, a small ration, in such a large room?"

"You nut. You mean the one with the Chinese rugs?"

"That one, yes. Where the sunlight is turning into wine."

"Tomorrow, Elio!" she shouted as he pulled away. Then much lower, so only she could hear, "I need you."

CHAPTER IX

"A drop more?" Jim said. "Made too much."

"A drop." Nancy had come home, gravitated to her favorite chair by the window, and was now, legs crossed, martini glass on the windowsill, fluffing her hair and sighing with the pleasure of being tiredly home.

Jim passed around behind her to pour, glad of the opportunity to contemplate with freedom the small, well-shaped head, slender neck, and close ears. From her South Carolina mother she had inherited her fine posture and good taste, from her Milanese father her high cheekbones, sharply perfect nose and occasional flashes of temper. More than once Jim had seen her father, a tiny import-export man with a penchant for the very best in clothes, liquor, food, candy and theater tickets, almost upset his wife's poise by doing something to her leg under the dinner table. And so it was with Nancy: the Italian in her under the table, the Southerner in her above it.

"Nancy, this letter was in the box when I came home." It was at times like this, when bad news seemed so gratuitous and out of place, that he wondered why he had ever wanted to be a doctor.

He had tried to be neither casual nor alarming, but this was his wife, not someone in one of Bellevue's wards, and just to look at her was to anticipate her reaction to the news. "Now, never mind the tears. Do you hear?"

Frightened, the blood leaving her face in its rush heartward, Nancy wouldn't take the letter, an airmail from Europe written on blue tissue paper that folded and became an envelope. "From Oona?"

"No. Dr. Maderini."

"Is she dead?"

"God damn it, read it, will you? Just read it. She isn't dead."

Nancy, whose father spoke English more or less as Maderini wrote it, might almost have been in Italy, in Maderini's office, as she read the letter, written in longhand with a pen that had obviously, and often, been dipped in ink.

Viale dei Platani, 26
Fiesole, Firenze, Italy
June 25, 1953

Dear Mr. & Mrs. James O'Hagen,

To write to you this letter is painful to my heart. All the same, it is to you that I must write. Oona talks about you. She reads me your letters, and it was from one of them that I copied your address.

At this time Oona is not a very healthy girl. She tells me that you are an intern, Mr. O'Hagen, so please let me say that on the day the baby is born, when I arrive at the villa, I am not alarmed by her condition. Hypertension, yes. Cardiac enlargement, yes. But in such a birth as this, what is abnormal may be normal. All the same, I have seen many premature babies, and always when one is like this baby, very small, *denutrito*, I say it has come out for food. The mother laughs when I say this, and I also laugh. But it is true. The food inside is not enough. Or it is turning bad. That is to say, the baby feels unwelcome. Something wrong. Instinct. So the baby leaves.

Also with your sister when I arrive at the villa, there is edema. Her ankles, her wrists, are swollen, and later, in my office, I find albumin in her urine.

Now it is many weeks later. Edema—gone. Blood chemistry—no abnormality. Kidney damage—little. But the blood pressure is still high. Lower, yes, but not enough lower. Also the albuminuria is still present. I did not see her until in the villa, after the baby. That is to say, nothing of medical history did I know. The headaches and the dizziness before the baby I did not know. Therefore, when she told me, later, of these things, and also that in America, as a girl, she had suffered scarlet fever, I decided that it was to you that I must write.

From the old scarlet fever, perhaps from some other infectious process, a bland form of chronic nephritis has developed in her body. From carrying the child the nephritic process started. I do not have proof of this, the afterbirth was normal, no lesion did I see, but of my diagnosis I have no doubt.

Oona does not know of this diagnosis, and I do not tell her. She would not be afraid, she has courage. But enough is enough. She wants to go home with her baby, and for that, for the trouble at the American Consulate, she needs all her strength.

In America perhaps she can be told. I tell you so that you will know what to do when she returns. That she is sick makes nothing to her. She says that she does not believe in sickness. Therefore, she is not a good patient. You know her. Also, you are American. Why does she not do as I ask? I do not ask something that is impossible. To eat and to rest is not impossible. You know, just simple food, good food. I do not mean filet mignon with artichoke sauce. Nothing with much style. Just food. Soft food. Little meat, in fact. Peasant food. Only no salt.

All my life I have many sick patients, many, even young patients like Oona. I know those who are to die, and they are the ones who always in the end die. Oona is the only wrong patient. She should be with those who are to die, but she is not. That is true because when I am with her, she makes me not worry. I try to worry, and to talk, but to listen to me, that is impossible for her. Whatever comes into her head, without delay it must come out. Otherwise, she thinks, it will be wasted. Do not be mistaken. I am her friend. But even with her face she talks. That is to say, if I am talking she talks with her face. And if she is not talking, she is writing letters. In short, excitement. No rest. She is lonely up here with her baby, and the baby cannot talk to her yet. I talk to her, but she does not listen, so with her I am no good.

Therefore, I beg you to do whatever is necessary to have her come home. In my machine I will drive her to Genova and take care until the ship sails. She will eat well on the ship, and talk, and probably rest. Then, in America, you will take care.

She is not in danger. That it is a bland form, an early form, I assure you. Also, with her God will be patient. With your Oona He will have to be.

I stop here, but I only want to say that as an old tree loves a bird bouncing among its branches, that is how I love her. She has a big heart and a mind that moves all over. Also she is very fine and she has much courage.

You have my respect, and my best wishes for everything that is good.

> *Cordially yours,*
> DR. ELIO MADERINI

"Is it hopeless?" Nancy said.

"What do you mean?"

"Why does God have to be patient?"

"You can't become run-down, he means. With any chronic disease that's true. Maderini's right, though. She should come home right away. I better get that letter about her 'husband' off to her right away. The one she wrote and asked me to copy."

"Why doesn't she go to the Consulate and admit the baby was born out of wedlock? Who cares, anyway?"

"She's going to have to be sent money in any case," Jim said. "So tomorrow—in the morning when no one's there—I'll drop in on my mother. I'll work on her, and she can work on my father. Incidentally, you said something once about going to the movies with Oona. Did it have anything to do with dill pickles?"

"How'd you know? Oona wouldn't go to a movie unless she brought a bag of dill pickles with her. Kind you get out of a barrel. I mean if she wore glasses, going to a movie without her pickles would be like going without her glasses. She'd bite into them little by little. Sort of suck on them all through the darn picture. It was amazing, how she could put those pickles away. Why?"

"Salt. There must have been something dormant there ever since the scarlet fever. Then the pregnancy. Strain on the kidneys. I told her, I begged her, to go to that hospital in Florence. The damn fool!"

CHAPTER X

The sign, "O'Hagen's Corner," extended at right angles around the four-story brick building whose sooty, curtainless windows bore the familiar "X" that meant the building was ripe for demolition. A sea-food truck had just dropped off cartons of lobster tails and shrimp, and now another truck was backing in with bags of Idaho potatoes and crated heads of lettuce. Except for O'Hagen's Corner, the bar and grill itself, there was a seared, black look about the place and a fumy smell from car and truck exhausts that annihilated all other smells. Skyscrapers rose so high and straight on all four sides that O'Hagen's Corner might have been something shiny—and possibly even precious—at the base of a huge incinerator shaft.

John O'Hagen, tall, with a kind face, a kind nature even, and a powerful, almost cruel-looking body, pushed out of a cab, or rather, pushed the cab away from him, and started around the vegetable truck to the entrance. Nine o'clock and the tables were already set. Good. Pile them in for lunch but save four tables for the regulars, the ones who remember the waiters at Christmas, show a little interest. "Nation of 'Fixers,' John, that's what we are," was the way a retired judge, an old uptown customer of O'Hagen's, had put it. "Want a ticket to a fight? Easy time with salesmen, cops, fire inspectors? All right, then remember this: The key word is 'fix.'"

A personal relationship, though, no. Not the same thing at all. O'Hagen had learned how to get along with the fixers, but in his personal relations he had never—until he'd taken over this bar and grill for Kevin—broken a trust or gone back on his word. His reputation as an honest business man, indeed, had been the deciding factor in his getting the bar and grill in the first place. Nat Feldman, an old friend and the owner of the property, had intended to raze the building and let the property lie fallow for a while after the war in 1945, until construction started again in New York. It was only when O'Hagen approached him about the possibility of renting the bar and grill without a lease (something the previous owner had refused to do) that Feldman changed his plans.

O'Hagen could pull out anytime he wanted if the business failed, Feldman said, but with the understanding that he *would* pull out, on short notice, if the tenement were to be razed for an office building. They further agreed that Feldman would receive a fixed monthly rent plus one-third of the monthly profits in excess of $1,500, these profits to be determined against expenses and salaries on the basis of the bar and table checks, which were to be numbered by the printer and stamped by the cash register as the money was rung up. This meant that only after salaries had been paid (Kevin's included) and John and Kevin O'Hagen had each made $750 a month in profits, would the owner begin to receive any additional revenue from the property.

In May, June, and July of 1946, after O'Hagen bought the fixtures from the previous owner and the sign had been changed to "O'Hagen's Corner," the total profits after expenses and salaries came to considerably less than $1,500 a month. All right, Kevin was out of his father's hair, he was making $75 a week in salary, and every month his share of the profits added up to a little more. Situated as they were at the very back door of the financial district, where literally thousands of people poured into the streets at lunchtime and where the imbibing of liquor during the lunch and cocktail hour was almost a prerequisite to success, it wasn't long before profits began to approach $1,500 a month.

John O'Hagen's original idea that they serve excellent food but a very simple menu, the same one every day, proved to be a great success and an easy one for Joe, the mammoth colored chef who stood at an exposed charcoal grill in the rear, to manage. They served three main dishes: charcoal-broiled club or T-bone steak, broiled lobster tails, and

jumbo shrimp broiled in garlic butter. With each
order an enormous baked Idaho potato was served
with butter, chives and sour cream, and an un-
limited amount of salad with a choice of dressings.
It was not an inexpensive place to eat, but John
O'Hagen's idea was to attract the kind of men
customers who were not concerned with price, and
in the end they were the kind of men who came. He
was so pleased that he agreed, when his son
broached the subject, to make Kevin a "legal"
partner and have new menus printed to read "O'Hagen & Son."

It was only after the partnership papers had been
signed and the profits began to exceed $1,500 a
month that the trouble between "O'Hagen & Son"
started. Kevin was making more money than he had
ever expected to make, from a business he had
criticized his father for setting up for him, a business
he had predicted would fail. But now, with Nat
Feldman's share of the profits adding up to more
each month, he devised a plan whereby two sets of
bar checks would be used, one set for the records,
another set for cutting the recorded profits above
$1,500 which Nat Feldman would share. From his
strategic position behind the very busy and always
noisy bar, it would be no problem for Kevin to
accept the money for the phony checks without
ringing them through the cash register. He would
use the phony checks only behind the bar, and only

on the big tippers, the steadies who looked at their checks, slapped down two, three or five dollars, and walked out with a wave without waiting for change.

"What's the *matter* with you, Kevin?" his father said when the subject was brought up. "I've known Nat Feldman for thirty-five years. He helped me get started. Now he's helping you. If it weren't for Nat, you wouldn't even *be* here."

"Listen, Pa. Wait. Look around and tell me what you see. Buildings, right? *Tall* buildings. *Sky*scrapers. In other words, real estate par excellence. Which means what, as far as this old tenement is concerned? Wrecking crews and steam shovels. Simple as that. Means they'll be building here in six months, a year, two at the most. That's all we've got here."

"What's our time here got to do with using phony bar checks? I made an agreement with Nat. I gave him my word. I've never gone back on my word, and I'm not starting now."

"We're *paying* him two thousand a month, aren't we? And we'll let him in on the profits too. I'm just thinking of an emergency fund, that's all. Insurance against bad days, like last summer—two weeks without an air conditioner. We still had to pay Feldman his two thousand, didn't we? And how much did *we* make while the air conditioner was being fixed?"

"Increase your salary, Kevin. Deduct two hundred

a month from my share and keep it. Only don't do anything with the checks. Do you hear?"

"What do you think I'm suggesting, Pa? That we keep *everything* over fifteen hundred? No! We use maybe twenty, thirty phony checks a day. No more than that. And you and I, we don't touch that money. We put it in a safe deposit box. It's there, for repairs, sickness in the family, an accident, things like that."

"I don't want to hear any more about it, Kevin. The answer's no. Now that's the end of it."

But the question of time, of how much longer they would *have* the bar and grill, of how many more monthly percentages would actually be forth-coming—a question which became more pressing with each passing day—made it impossible for Kevin to leave his father alone. His father didn't work there, and that bothered Kevin too. He, not his father, had to dig into ice cubes all day long, summer and winter. He, not his father, had to go from one end of the bar to the other all day, making this, that, and the other kind of drink, the cus-tomer's men and brokers, noblesse oblige bastards, thinking they were superior! While all his father did was collect!

And so he nagged his father, at home in the evening, at the bar in the morning—nagged him as only Kevin could nag another human being. Week after week he spoke of nothing else—if he spoke at all. At all other times he wore such a hurt, long-suffering expression that his father, who could no more stand peevish silence in a room than he could talkativeness in a theater, invariably asked, "All right, all right! What's eating you now?"

"I'm not supposed to talk about it, Pa. You told me not to talk about it. So let's not talk about it."

"That phony-check idea of yours all we have to talk about? You have a wife and four daughters. Why don't you talk about them?"

"Exactly. Why don't I, Pa? You tell me. I don't talk about them because I'm thinking about them, their future . . ." The midday crowd had left and they were in a booth by the window where the waiters couldn't hear them. They had ordered a steak apiece and were waiting to be served, so naturally Kevin had to make matters worse by indulging in that habit of his of straightening out the silverware, his own and his father's. Knives, forks, spoons—everything had to be absolutely parallel, especially now that they were back on his favorite theme, the rationale of his existence.

"I told you last time, Kevin. Leave my silverware alone."

"All right. Don't get sore."

"I'm not sore. Just leave it alone."

"All right. I'm sorry. I'll leave your silverware alone. But about the bar, Pa. I'm down here. I see

what's going on. I know they'll be building here
soon. Not tomorrow. Not the next day. But soon.
And the point is—you said it yourself—I have a wife
and four daughters. Bachelor, I wouldn't give a
damn. Married but no children, even, I wouldn't
give a damn. As things stand, though, I've got
various and sundry reasons—"

It went on this way, endlessly, week after week,
until finally John O'Hagen, old and weary enough
to lean heavily on Kevin's reasoning that it would
only be for a few months, gave in to his son. And so
just as he had, on the strength of his honesty, ob-
tained the bar and grill for Kevin, so now he was
allowing Kevin, for the sake of "a few months," to
destroy the quiet pride that for him had naturally
gone with being honest.

It was a decision O'Hagen never got over. Lying
awake at night, he thought, worried about it; going
about his business during the day, he wondered
what had happened to him. Too old-fashioned to
believe a man can be made to do what he doesn't
want to do, he only occasionally lashed out in his
thoughts at Kevin. In the end he blamed himself,
and in dimly lit bars around the city he began to
drink more, to tip more, to say "Thank you,"
"Excuse me" more. To Maggie he said nothing,
preferring to compound the original wrong than to
lose his wife's respect. On the other hand, he never
went near the safe deposit box either, never used

any of the money in it, never spoke to Kevin about
it. Then in 1952 after his heart attack, with three
heart specialists telling him "to slow down," with
the lease on his own bar and grill running out, and
Columbia University, in the throes of a post-war
expansion program, reluctant to renew it, he had
retired from business and begun to live entirely on
his share of the profits from O'Hagen's Corner.

Kevin's prediction that the business would last
"two years at the most" had been as wrong as his
earlier prediction that in the financial district another bar and grill "could not possibly succeed."
This did not prevent him, however, from talking
about the imminent end of the business. On the
contrary, the longer it lasted the more he insisted—
the more he was impelled to insist—that it didn't
have much longer to go. "Won't be long now," he'd
say to his mother, father, wife—anyone who'd listen.
"Surveyors all over the place yesterday. Maybe
another month, two at the most, and the place'll be
finished."

More grasping the wealthier he became, he was
afraid that Jim, Oona, Cathy and the others, who
were after all John O'Hagen's children too, might
begin asking where they came in, why one and only
one of the seven children should get everything. So
the fiction of the bar's imminent end went on. It
was impossible for the children to drop by to see
their parents without being told the "latest" on the

business's precarious existence.

Now it was seven years later, and the weekly deposits of untaxed and untaxable money were still accumulating in a safe deposit box accessible only to the two "legal" partners. If one partner died, the other partner and no one else would know how much was in it, or even that it existed. Not only that, but according to the partnership papers Kevin had had drawn up, the surviving partner would automatically become the sole owner of the business, so that if John O'Hagen died first (and he was 72, Kevin 37), the six other children would have no way of dividing their father's half of the business among them.

O'Hagen found Kevin behind the bar, and as an opener, so seldom did he drop by this early in the morning, threw out, "Tables set already, Kevin, I see. Those brokers and customer's men, fellows on the Exchange—they really know about the place now, don't they?"

"Eighty-six, seven, eight, nine—ninety . . . What'd you say, Pa? I'm trying to finish this."

"Nothing. Go ahead." He didn't work here. Retired. All right, and the count did have to be exact. Not only that, the checks themselves had to be tabulated and kept in a batch to corroborate each day's entry in the book. Kevin was good at figures, though, and almost never made a mistake. He also had an excellent memory for things like telephone numbers, baseball batting averages, the number of American dead and wounded on Guadalcanal, and Ike's state-by-state plurality over Adlai Stevenson. The night those returns came in, O'Hagen remembered it so well. Kevin and Oona happened to be at the house together, Kevin with his "I-Like-Ike" button, a score-sheet and pencil, and Oona, a Stevenson buff, just listening. Finally, because the greater the Eisenhower lead the more Kevin did his figuring aloud, Oona turned to him and said, "Why the arithmetic, Kevin? Don't you know that anything you can do, Univac can do better?" Her other remark, about how Ike's upraised arms reminded her of Al Jolson singing "Swanee"—well, Kevin had asked for it, calling Stevenson "a sawed-off Lincoln with a pear-shape." That was Kevin, though. Derivative. Nothing original.

"What was that you just said, Pa? About customer's men?"

"Wasn't important. Nothing."

"Well, what was it anyway? Now I'm through counting, it's a secret?"

"I said they know about the place now, that's all. That's all I said." He had something on his mind and Kevin, as usual, bothered him, would not respond, could not look happy. Ever since his heart attack he'd tried to keep peace with this oldest son of his, this "partner" whose face and voice came alive only when he was nagging, complaining, criticizing. Nothing was ever right, nothing ever gave him joy, nothing but cruelty—the humor of the gutter—ever made him laugh.

"Kevin, I want to talk to you about something and I don't want any shouting. You hear? I don't need your permission to do what I want to do, but I'd be pleased if you'd agree with me."

"Is it about the emergency fund?"

O'Hagen, sitting on a bar stool (the chef and waiters were in the kitchen), looked up at his son's pompadour of blond hair, the blond eyebrows and blue eyes, the rosy cheeks—a handsome American with a small soul, a scared-eager look on his face. "What made you say that?"

"Irregardless. It's too late to do anything about the fund now. We can't split it with Feldman, if that's what you're driving at. I didn't expect the business to last this long and neither did you. We split with him now, he may have us both locked up. Your privilege, what you think of him. I'm not even saying you're wrong. I just wouldn't want to take the chance."

"Relax, Kevin. I'm not talking about Feldman or doing away with the fund." But wasn't he becoming more and more like Kevin if he couldn't resist telling him to "relax"? Was this what it was like to be Kevin? How awful. "Your mother and I received a letter this morning. Oona's baby, the one she said she adopted—"

"What's the emergency fund got to do with Oona?"

"Will you let me finish? She didn't adopt a baby in Italy. She *had* a baby."

"Oh, my God, that girl—that girl! She'll disgrace this family yet. Mark my words, Pa. Before she's through, we'll all have to move from the neighborhood."

O'Hagen wondered what they would all have to do if the emergency fund ever came to light, but he didn't speak of that. He wanted to do something for Oona, wanted Kevin's cooperation. "Wait a minute. She's married."

"She is?" Kevin blushed at how quick he had been to assume the worst. But wasn't it only natural? Wasn't he justified? Oona O'. No "Hagen" for Oona. Oh no. Apostrophe, that's all, which was what she really was, a goddamn female apostrophe who showed him no respect, was not afraid of him, thought of him as some kind of joke! "She's married? Well, then, fine, Pa. She's married. I'm married. You're married. We're all married."

"Or at least she was."

"Was? What in God's name did she do—get divorced already? Wasn't she even married in church?"

"I don't know about that. She was married last September in Maryland, to a man named Peter Penhaligan. He died four months ago in New York.

Some disease with a long name I never heard of."

"Some disease with a long name you never heard of? Only Oona's husband could die of a disease you never heard of."

"Stop it, will you, Kevin? She knew about the disease—maybe you do too—I just can't remember the name now. He was with the U.N. Used to travel a lot through Central and South America." He waited a moment, hopeful that Kevin would soften toward his sister and want to help her. Instead of that Kevin began to use his mind and frown, like a man trying to find a way out of a trap. "How much is in the emergency fund, Kevin?"

Not since the start of the fund had the subject, let alone the accumulated amount, been mentioned between them.

"Why? You call Oona an emergency? That girl who's never lifted her finger to help you and Mama, never brought a penny home, never done anything but have fun?"

"You didn't answer my question."

"You have as much right to that deposit box as I do, Pa. I haven't counted it. Interesting question, though. Didn't her husband have any insurance? Or do people at the U.N. expect America to pay for their personal bills as well? We've been suckers for that goldbrick outfit of Roosevelt's all along. And because this husband of Oona's worked there— 'worked,' pardon me—does that give him the right to make her a sucker, you a sucker, me a sucker?"

"Is it important now whether he had insurance or not? If your sister is in need of help? Don't you want to help her? Can't you understand my wanting to?"

"Pa, I don't have to be a genius to understand your wanting to. Ever since that girl was born . . . I remember it so well. Amsterdam Avenue. Five flights of stairs. Opening up the beds at night. And Oona? Why, that darling little blonde with all the curls, nothing but the best. Your favorite. She's always been your favorite."

"Then why didn't I set her up in business instead of you? Why didn't I make her a partner? Why didn't I sign papers giving her this business when I die? What will she get when that happens? And what will you?"

"What's she ever done? I work part time going to school. Full time the moment I get out. Right up to the war I work, and Mama gets everything I make— everything, except ten dollars a week."

Suddenly O'Hagen felt tired and at his son's disposal, available to him as one is to the desperate. Why, though, did the child who bitched the most— at least in this family—always get the most? The others, and Jim and Oona especially, had never assumed they had anything "coming to them," and now with his heart attack, his own business gone, and only this bar and grill left, nothing *would* be coming to them—or to Cathy either, who wasn't even married, out of college, yet.

"I'm not taking what you did away from you, Kevin. But you're the oldest. I wasn't doing well then. The depression . . ."

"Don't I know, Pa? You think I don't know about the depression? The point is, does *Oona?*"

"Why should she? She came later. She was brought up differently."

"That's putting it mildly. And Jim's another one. And now Cathy. They're three of a kind. Fun, fun, fun. That's all they think of. Fooling around and having fun."

"I never asked you not to go to college," O'Hagen said. Because that's what Kevin was really doing, talking about college. In fact, if Kevin deserved forgiveness, it was because Jim and Oona had gone and he hadn't. Bright, a fast thinker, argumentative and overbearing, he might have made a very good prosecuting attorney.

"Did you ever ask me *to* go, Pa? Did you have the money to send me?"

"No, and I'm sorry about that. But I didn't ask Jim to go either. For that matter, I didn't have the money to send him. He just went."

"On scholarship? Who can't go on scholarship?"

"You played football in high school too, didn't you, Kevin?"

"No All-Scholastic, though, is that it? I didn't make it so I didn't get to prep school with a bunch of wealthy bastards. Wall Street bastards park their cars here. Was that my fault?"

"No, it wasn't your fault. It was no one's fault." It wasn't easy, even when you believed in luck, as John O'Hagen did, to be father to this son. Life was unfair. Some people did get more, and others less, than they deserved. But bad luck would never explain, or excuse, in John O'Hagen's eyes, anyone's being a bastard. Kevin had come into the world this way, or at least with a great capacity for being this way. Bad luck, the world, had had only as much to do with it as he'd allowed. And the same with the others. Hadn't Jim been a stutterer all through grammar and high school? If not for football and the way he'd "expressed" himself in scrimmage, he might still be a stutterer. And if not for his being a stutterer to begin with, he might never have made All-Scholastic and gone to college. No, it was a mystery why people were what they were, and to O'Hagen's way of thinking, it would always be a mystery.

"Kevin, I want you to go to the bank and get five hundred dollars from that safe deposit box. Oona needs the money and I want to send it to her."

"Simple, Pa. The bank's eight blocks from here. Go and get it."

"You've gone every week for seven years. I've

never gone, and I don't want to go." The mere thought of the safe deposit box, tucked in a wall in an old mahogany-paneled bank where crisp Anglo-Saxons wearing derbies did their business, made John O'Hagen blush. But he needed the money for Oona. His daughter needed it.

"You go in with your key, Pa. You identify yourself. You sign a slip. The guard shows you where it is. Nothing to it, and besides, I'm busy. I work here. While Oona gallivants in Europe, I work here. But she needs five hundred and you want to give it to her. Fine. Go over and get it for her."

"You refuse to get the money for me?"

"No, I don't refuse to get it for you. I refuse to get it for Oona. Your heart attack last year, what'd I do? Did I go to the hospital and ask you how much you wanted?"

"And what'd I say?"

"You said you didn't want anything. You had enough to pay the doctor and hospital, you said. But did I ask?"

His father looked at him and stood up. Human decency called for only one response from Kevin, and already he had found a "reasonable" obstruction to put in the way of it. His distrust and resentment of Oona, his envy of Jim, his older-generation annoyance with Cathy, constituted the real impulse behind his desire for money and power. He wanted what they had, and what they had was a mystery. Money could not buy it and he was fool enough, miser enough, to think that money could. All you needed was *enough* money. And what *was* enough? Kevin didn't know. He never would know.

"Oona's U.N. man didn't have any insurance, you said. Well, listen to this, and don't forget it. I don't have any insurance either, and if anything happens to me, half of what's in that box is your mother's."

"I know *that*, Pa. What'd you think, I'd—"

"Shup *up!* And how we got it. You don't tell her that, either. Just give it to her. We saved it. Put it in a bank in the neighborhood in *her* name, so she can go there *herself* when she needs it. You hear?"

"Of course, Pa—"

But O'Hagen had walked out, an old man still not used to his new dishonesty. At the corner he hailed a cab. "Central Hanover. Corner of—"

But when the cab pulled up to the bank and he got out, he walked past the entrance to the next corner. On his second try he hesitated, looked in through the window. Then on to the opposite corner. He passed back and forth several times, stopping each time and looking in, then walking on again. He tried very hard but could not bring himself to enter. That locked box contained the proof of his disintegration as a man, and not even for Oona, whom he dearly loved, could he unlock it.

. . . And back at O'Hagen's Corner, Kevin's wife
Lucille and his two youngest daughters, Veronica
and Nora, were stopping by on their way to Wana-
maker's. Kevin immediately recognized the second-
hand Cadillac he'd bought at a steal from a friend
of his father's and went around the bar to the entrance to greet them. Lucille, a tall, slender girl
from the mountains of New Hampshire, had that
weather-beaten American look one associates with
political campaigns, civic-mindedness, and baked-
bean dinners in armories where about a thousand
people make speeches.

"Kevin, what's the matter?" she said. "Are they
going to build?"

She too had been so conditioned by Kevin's talk
of the bar's imminent demise that whenever he
looked troubled she immediately got visions of
construction workers drilling long dynamite holes
into the massive veins of granite beneath the building.

But before Kevin could answer his two daughters
were climbing all over him. Veronica, five and the
older of the two, had reached his shoulders first
and, while holding on to his hair, was trying to prevent her sister from sharing the "top of the mountain" with her.

"No, they're not building, Lucille. *Oona's* coming home, that's all."

Saying Oona made him look angry, but it had

nothing to do with his two daughters, who were almost literally tearing him apart in their efforts to
get to the "top of the mountain." Oona, in fact,
who had never been to Kevin's apartment, was
hopelessly mistaken about Kevin's domination over
his children. The exact opposite was true, and
Kevin, as though never loved and now overwhelmed
by his love for them and theirs for him, could do
absolutely nothing to chastise or control them. He
wanted nothing to happen to this one miracle in
his life, his love for his wife and daughters, wanted
the whole world shut out from it, wanted nothing
to threaten it.

"Veronica, Nora, please. You're ripping Daddy's
shirt!"

"It's all right. Don't yell at my babies. They want
to get to the top of the mountain." Then he shook
his head in disgust. "How do you like that Oona,
though. Coming home with a baby!"

CHAPTER XI

On August 2, when Oona received the letter from Jim about her "husband," she immediately got in touch with Dr. Maderini, who said he would drive her to the Consulate the next day. She had expected to be overjoyed at the prospect of obtaining a passport for her daughter, but the letter, which Jim had merely copied and sent back addressed to "Mrs. Anthony O'Hagen," had the exact opposite effect. It depressed her (she *had* no husband), worried her (would the plan *work?*), and worst of all, revived what she had been trying to forget ("You should handle your affairs more intelligently, Miss O'Hagen").

When Mrs. Friedensohn had made that remark, she had either been telling her to eat cake, or saying in effect that there was no difference between them, that Oona could handle her affairs as intelligently without money as Mrs. Friedensohn could with it. There was a difference between them, though, and Oona knew it wasn't money so much as the lifetime habit of having or not having money at your disposal. She could inherit a fortune and she still wouldn't handle her affairs intelligently. The habit

of being frantic was too ingrained; she couldn't
break that habit now even with a million dollars.
She'd be frantically rich instead of frantically
poor—but still frantic. Just as Mrs. Friedensohn
couldn't break the habit of being calm and collected
even with all her money gone. If poverty became
too cumbersome for her and she decided to take
poison, she would use one of her best glasses and
take it in little Drambuie sips. Oona would gulp
hers down right out of the bottle, but not Mrs.
Friedensohn—she would be stemware-conscious to
the very end.

The next day was a critical one for Oona, a day
full of nervousness, uncertainty, and disruptive emotions. It being August, the American Consulate, a
government office not to be denied its share of
inefficiency even during the slack season, was
jammed with American tourists. They were in the
hallways, on the stairs, filing in and out of this or
that office, men in wildly printed shirts and women
in linen, camera-armed college boys and freshly
starched little girls—compatriots all in this musty,
down-at-heel building that belonged to, was part of,
the good old U.S.A.

For Oona, who was supposed to have had an
appointment, it was a place of confinement, pro-
cedural nonsense, and neglect. Rattled by the noise
and constantly reminded of her predicament by
how happy every other American looked, she sat

with Maderini as if in a void between the person she
had been before she had arrived and the person she
was going to be the moment she left. Government
offices did that to her anyway; in fact, she had never
collected unemployment insurance for that reason.
She hated being the person—or rather, the non-
person—in between.

When finally her name was called and she entered
a smaller and much quieter inner office, the aliena-
tion persisted. She felt incidental to what was going
on even though, in this office at least, she was the
subject of what was going on. Not that she had ever
thought of herself as being important to the government—on the contrary, it was just that she had
never before thought of herself vis-à-vis her own
country. She was not a criminal, she had never had
any trouble with the law, and yet here she was—
extenuating circumstances notwithstanding—trying
to commit a fraud. All right, Uncle Sam had the
wherewithal for something like that, and what
counted was the wherewithal, not the fraud, or even
the person trying to commit it. She was the person
trying to commit it, though, which was what made
her hate being so incidental to, and yet the object
of, the Consulate's wherewithal.

Maderini entered the smaller office with her, and
luckily the vice-consul wasn't there. The man taking
his place, a Mr. McAllister, said, "Oh, yes," when
she introduced herself, and got her folder from a

(162)

drawer in the vice-consul's desk.

After introducing Maderini as her doctor and pediatrician, she explained the reason for her coming, said it was very important that she leave for the United States immediately, and handed him Jim's letter, which read as follows:

Dear Oona,

I've just received your letter, and I must say you sound very depressed and lonely. You ask why Anthony hasn't written, why he hasn't joined you, why everyone in the family skirts around your questions about him. Well, though the rest of the family think it best to keep silent, I think you should be told the truth.

Anthony has been in the hospital for the past month. And while his condition is not critical (he was in an automobile accident), it is such that he cannot write or join you at present. I visited him today (he's at St. Luke's) and this letter is the result.

If I were you, Oona, I'd come home with the baby. You're obviously not happy in Italy, Anthony needs you, and I know you'd much prefer being with him and your family (everybody, incidentally, is very anxious to see the baby).

I don't, however, want this letter to frighten you. As I said, Anthony is in no danger; he would just

like to see the baby and have you with him. You say
your maid's been ill and you're unable to leave the
villa, so it wouldn't be as though you were cutting
short a sightseeing tour of Italy. You're alone, and
he's alone, so get your plane ticket, tell me your
flight number, and I'll be at Idlewild to meet
you.

Your brother,
JIM

Oona had never written herself a letter before,
and seeing it in McAllister's hands, watching his
face as he read what might have been but was not
true, caught her with her self-image down. She saw
herself with imagination as someone to be pitied,
felt pity for herself for being pitiful. And yet
because her plan called for complete, if not peremp-
tory, assurance on her part, she put her passport, the
ten-dollar fee for her daughter's passport, and two
photos of her daughter on McAllister's desk before
he had even finished reading the letter. She was
"taking it for granted," in other words, that under
the circumstances, with her husband incapacitated
in a hospital in New York, there would be no
question of her daughter's being given a passport.
But it was precisely at this point, while she was
trying to impose upon and deceive McAllister, that
she saw herself as Mrs. Friedensohn had seen her,

pregnant, unmarried and without money, that afternoon at the villa.

Caught in the same predicament, in America say,
Mrs. Friedensohn would never have gone to the
Italian Consulate this way, with so few alternatives
at her disposal, depending only on some lucky turn
of wit, the kindness of an official, a momentary lack
of discipline. Of course without money Oona had
had no way of obtaining legal advice, but even so,
and even without money, Mrs. Friedensohn would
not have done it this way. What *would* she have
done? Oona wished she knew. Indeed, if Mrs.
Friedensohn were the author of a book entitled,
"How To Handle Your Affairs Intelligently," Oona
would long since have bought and studied it.

"Mrs. O'Hagen, when did you receive this letter
from your brother?" McAllister said.

"This morning."

"And your brother's last name is—?"

"Penhaligan. James Michael Penhaligan."

"I see," he said, and picked it up to look at it
again.

Oona thought she'd won, so she added, with as
much relief as magnanimity, "I packed immediately
and called the airport, but then realized I was—well,
putting the cart before the horse, so to speak, calling
for reservations before coming here."

"I can appreciate what this means to you, Mrs.
O'Hagen," McAllister said, "but this letter, by

itself, does not permit me to issue your daughter a passport."

"But I have to leave, and I can't leave *without* my daughter."

"Do you happen to know the serial number of your husband's passport? I could cable Washington and have his citizenship verified in a matter of hours."

"Goodness," Oona said (and it was true), "I don't know the number of my own passport, and it's right there on your desk."

Disappointed, McAllister began tapping the eraser end of his pencil on the desk. Oona could see that he was trying hard to help her, but officials who tried as hard as he was trying were the most dangerous. If McAllister had a wife and six children, and they all had passports, he would have known the serial number of each one. He was that kind of man—a Corporal Eisenhower with a good memory.

"Could you cable your brother?" he said.

"Yes, of course. Why?"

"Well, if he could send over your husband's birth certificate, his Army discharge papers, something of that sort, I could issue your daughter a passport immediately."

"But my husband doesn't have papers of that sort at the hospital with him. My brother would have to ask him for the keys to our apartment, and tell him why he wanted them. My husband is worried enough about me as it is. He'd be *furious* with my brother for upsetting me."

Maderini and the Italian assistant had been looking from McAllister to Oona, from Oona to McAllister. Now, however, on what almost seemed a signal between them, they began looking only at McAllister. Though neither said a word, it became obvious to Oona, and apparently to McAllister too, that they were trying to pressure him into giving her what she wanted. Italians were very Madonna conscious, but in a way that *added*, if anything, Oona thought, to their relations with women. A mother to them was a flower in a pot, a girl a flower in the field. They loved and adored the flowers in the field (no one had to tell her that the world's worst wolves were in Italy), but they *respected* the flowers in pots and were personally offended if anyone showed disrespect. McAllister wasn't doing that, he just wasn't being corrupt enough to suit the two Italians.

"Mrs. O'Hagen, I'm sorry," McAllister said, his Yankee rectitude bristling against the pressure of the two Italians. "I'm deeply sorry, but under the provisions of Section 301, Subsection (a) Item (3) of the Immigration and Nationality Act of 1952, positive proof of the United States citizenship of both parents is required."

But Mr. McAllister, one moment, please,"

Oona said. "Can you prove my husband *isn't* a citizen?"

It was a stupid thing to say and she *knew* it was stupid, but the impulse to prove Mrs. Friedensohn right on the one hand, and to free herself of the responsibility of getting her daughter back to America on the other, had become irresistible. She didn't know why Mrs. Friedensohn had come back to plague her this way, except that she had always associated Mrs. Friedensohn's interest in the baby with her own desire to make the baby an American citizen—with her fear, that is, that as long as the baby's status remained indefinite, Mrs. Friedensohn might get the baby away from her. At any rate, she knew Mrs. Friedensohn would have *expected* her to be stupid and she wanted at all costs, at that moment, to be comprehensible to Mrs. Friedensohn. The whole thing seemed illogical and crazy even to Oona, but just the *thought* of Mrs. Friedensohn's being shocked at her saying something intelligent precluded her saying it. It was as if she *wanted* to lose her baby, but she knew the exact opposite was true. Why else did she always dream of Sheila's dying and then, on waking, become overwhelmingly relieved to find her alive? Why, if not that Mrs. Friedensohn made up the dream part, and Sheila's American citizenship the waking part?

"I'm very sorry, Mrs. O'Hagen," McAllister was

saying, "but it is not the Consulate's responsibility to prove the truth of your statements. It is your responsibility to supply the Consulate with proof."

Going off on another tack, this one only slightly more intelligent than the last, Oona said, "Please look at my passport, Mr. McAllister. Is it positive proof that I'm a citizen of the United States?"

He picked it up and looked at it much more carefully, Oona thought, than was necessary. "Yes, Mrs. O'Hagen, but not that your husband is."

"Very well, then," Oona said. "Section 309, Subsection (c) of our Immigration and Nationality Act," and she got her copy from her handbag, "reads, and I quote, 'Notwithstanding the provision of subsection (a) of this section, a person born, on or after the effective date of this Act, outside the United States and out of wedlock shall be held to have acquired at birth the nationality status of his or her mother, if the mother had the nationality of the United States at the time of such person's birth, and if the mother had previously been physically present in the United States or one of its outlying possessions for a continuous period of one year.' "

McAllister started to speak, but Oona interrupted him. "Please let me finish, Mr. McAllister. Now since my passport is positive proof that I'm an American citizen, and since my daughter's Italian birth certificate, also on your desk, is positive proof that she is my daughter, I meet the requirements of the section I just quoted."

"But Mrs. O'Hagen, you're married."

"But you just said I have no proof that my husband is a citizen of the United States. I do, however, have proof that I am a citizen, and also that Sheila O'Hagen is my child. Since you give me no choice, I must ask you to approve the Consular Report of Birth and the Certification of Birth in accordance with the proof I *do* have. I have to return with my child to my husband immediately, and if this is the only way I can do it, then I'll do it this way and have the Certification of Birth corrected when I get back and my husband leaves the hospital."

There was one flaw in this argument, and McAllister found it. Oona had been trying to save face, but he wasn't even going to let her do that.

"Mrs. O'Hagen, you cannot tell me one minute that you're married, and ask me the next minute to approve the Consular Report of Birth on the basis of an entirely different set of requirements. You would be perjuring yourself to say your child was born out of wedlock, and I would be approving what I knew to be a false report."

"All right, then!" Oona shouted, for this was what always happened when she tried to handle her affairs with even a little intelligence. Everything got jammed up and she had to blast her way out in the end anyhow. "I'm not married. I was lying. I have no husband. But the baby *is* mine and I'm an American citizen, so please approve the forms so I can go home!"

"To your husband?"

He was really a bastard, when you came right down to it. No one could stick that close to the book and be anything else. "No! To my mother and father!"

Reduced this way to telling the truth, and yet believed less than when she had been lying, she started to cry. It was the right time to cry if she was going to cry at all, but now all pretense was gone, she wasn't trying to deceive him any more, she didn't want to cry, she was just crying. And yet as she turned away with Maderini's handkerchief in her hand (it was silk and she hated soiling it), she found herself saying almost with cunning to herself, "Everything that happens is like the person it happens to." If she hadn't broken down it un-doubtedly would not have happened, but on the outside she was shaking violently, and on the inside she was saying very calmly to herself, "Everything that happens is like the person it happens to." At the same time, as though her mind had a bleacher section, she was quite a distance from it all, thinking of Aldous Huxley's *Point Counter Point*. She hadn't read it for years, but she was positive she had read that in *Point Counter Point*, and what she couldn't get over—regardless of where she'd read it—was the way it tied in with, or rather, contradicted, Mrs. Friedensohn's belief that a lifetime of wealth didn't make any difference.

Oona completely agreed with Huxley and she was sure that if she could become invisible and follow Mrs. Friedensohn through the rest of her life, everything that happened to Mrs. Friedensohn, no matter how small or insignificant, would be exactly like Mrs. Friedensohn. What she had to keep in mind, if Huxley was right (and he had to be, coming from a family like that), was the simple question: Did she want what happened to Mrs. Friedensohn to happen to her? If not (and she didn't), then she should simply be herself and let her own things happen to her.

She had other thoughts too, but the best one of all was how she already knew where, in her dresser drawer at home, she was going to keep Maderini's handkerchief. She was going to ask him if she could keep it, of course, but there she was, still crying, still pitting Aldous Huxley against Mrs. Friedensohn, and at the same time thinking of the handkerchief all washed and ironed and carefully tucked away in her dresser drawer in New York.

Mr. McAllister, meanwhile, had begun to write something on the Certification of Birth. Oona thought he was voiding the whole thing, but then, shaking his head judiciously, he said, "In my thirty years with the foreign service, I've never been confronted with anything like this."

When no one said anything, he seemed disappointed. Nevertheless, he signed his name and
pressed the Consulate's seal into the paper itself.

"Now, Mrs. O'Hagen, rather than have you go
through a great deal of trouble when you get home,
I've approved these forms, with notations, as they
stand. As for your child's passport, I can amend
yours, if you wish, to include your daughter. There's
no charge for that, and you and your daughter will
have no trouble traveling together. Most mothers
with infants travel with amended passports."

"Amend mine, then, please," Oona said, and
thought, Found money.

Finally, as he handed her the amended passport,
the Certification of Birth, and the ten dollars, he
said, "Have a safe trip and good luck."

From the way he smiled as he said it, Oona could
tell that he really believed that with the possible
exception of Will Rogers, who was dead anyway, he
was the pleasantest guy in the world. She was
supposed to be pleasant too, only she had glanced at
the notation he'd written on the Certification of
Birth ("Neither marriage license nor proof of father's citizenship submitted"), so she found it a
little hard to be. Not that she was unpleasant, she
just asked him, that's all, "Mr. McAllister, were you
ever an air-raid warden?"

It was a long shot, but she was good at long shots.

In fact, if she were to lay down a challenge to Mrs. Friedensohn, it would be to a long-shot contest.

"Matter of fact, I was," McAllister said. "Why, were you with the auxiliaries during the war? You're too young."

"No, you just remind me of the warden in our block, that's all."

"I do?" The idea, small as it was, seemed to please him no end.

"You also remind me of the warden in the block next to ours," Oona went on. "And the warden in the block next to that. You remind me of him too."

"Why, were they triplets, or something?" Three and one made four. That made four McAllisters in that one area alone. He was on the verge of giggling.

"They might have been triplets, I'm not sure," Oona said. "Their armbands and helmets and whistles were all the same, though." She smiled. "Amazing, isn't it? Why don't you sit there and think about it awhile?"

Out in the street, she took Maderini's arm and walked for a long time without speaking. She had overprepared herself for the Consulate, given the whole mess her complete attention for weeks, and now felt exhausted and let down. And yet (take her "and yets" away and she'd lose the whole trick of living), there was Maderini walking beside her with that same captain-of-the-ship expression on his face. She knew he was thinking about her, and so loved him all the more for not abandoning his old wreck of a ship. If he had changed his way of walking then, she would have felt even less secure than she did. As it was, McAllister's notation became something like "dirty weather," and as every captain knew, that was something you were bound to meet up with at sea. She looked up at him and smiled, for he was that very rare person, a true gentleman, and no matter what else ever happened to her, she would always remember him and always treasure his handkerchief. Very few people were so innately good that they had nothing to do with morals, and he was one of them. Not once, not even for an instant, had she gotten the feeling that he thought less of her for not handling her affairs intelligently.

CHAPTER XII

Via C Angelico 5
Villa Roseto
Fiesole, Firenze, Italy
August 10, 1953

Dear Jim and Nancy,

This is it—at last! I have my provisional ticket (the Vulcania, sailing from Genoa August 23rd and arriving in New York September 5th) and Mama and Papa's okay. I'm taking a ship rather than a plane to see if I can gain a little weight before anybody sees me. Sheila is costing $10, and she'll drink that much in milk alone.

As for the trip from here to Genoa, Dr. Maderini has *insisted* upon driving us. What a guy, I swear, and am I going to *miss* him. I've begged him, selfishly, to visit America, but he says he's too old. I love him, I really do. Life is so deep, so sweet, so warm, when he's around, and I'm such a nicer person than I am ordinarily. If things don't work out in New York, maybe I can come back here and be his secretary, or his "crazy American," whichever he'd prefer.

Maria just came in with your letter about the

Magnavox. I don't know what to say, how to thank you, any more. I didn't expect you to go down and *speak* to the people at Altman's about the Magnavox for me. They'd call and tell you their decision, I thought, and you'd abide by it. I can imagine the trouble you had, though I had a hunch they'd agree. They're really very kind; I've always liked that store. Just before I left for Italy I canceled a beautiful cocoa rug and they didn't say a word.

The check (and thank goodness the loss is so little) is made out to Mrs. Anthony Friedensohn, so I'm sending it back to you immediately, endorsed for deposit in your account. As soon as it clears your bank, cable the money to me, Oona O'Hagen (the name on my passport), in care of the American Express office in Florence, so I can have it changed into travelers' checks.

Deduct the cost of the cable and fifty dollars from the total, and have dinner and see a show on me. Have you ever been to Le Valois on 58th Street? The food is excellent, and if you want to linger over cocktails (or over coffee afterward) they don't rush you.

As for the furniture, you're absolutely right. It would be ridiculous to sell it for $500 when I may eventually, as I said in an earlier letter, have to set up an apartment with some girls.

As soon as I get those travelers' checks, I'm coming, ready or not. There's nothing keeping me

here any longer anyway, now that I've got Mama
and Papa's okay. Mama wrote me herself about it,
on lined paper in her own handwriting, and just as
you'd expect, she writes the way she talks.

"Oona," she starts off by saying (and I could
almost *hear* her), "why do you always have to go
one better than the truth? I couldn't *believe* you'd
adopt a baby at your age. Why did you say you did?
Do you think your father and I know so little about
life that we can't be told the truth when one of our
children gets into trouble? You're our daughter and
nothing will ever change that. So come home with
your baby and we'll manage somehow . . ." And so
on. Then she goes on to say that Cathy wrote the
letters for her because of her eyes. "You *know*
they're bad, Oona—not that I can't see through
you . . ." And so on.

Remember Mama's grocery lists when we were
kids, Jim, how the youngest child always had to get
used to the old-fashioned way she made certain
letters? Well, what she *said* didn't make me cry, but
the handwriting did—those old-fashioned letters.
Just seeing them was like walking down Amsterdam
Avenue into the A & P. The old store, I mean,
remember? Where the hand-worn wooden counters
felt smooth and nice even against your chin?

Another thing. Papa just sent me $200 in care of
the American Express office in Florence. A long
time ago, before I even thought of trying to return

the Magnavox, I asked him for my fare home, but he never answered. I mean until yesterday, and then all he said was, "If this isn't enough, Oona, let me know. But come home. Your mother and I are waiting for you." I didn't want to ask him for money and I hope he knows that. Anyway, now that you've returned the Magnavox, I'll be able to pay him back.

Now don't forget, on September 5th, call the Italian lines and get the arrival time. I'll be coming down the gangplank with Sheila in my arms and I want you two to *be* there. I'm counting on it. Then we can all go up to Mama and Papa's. Maybe not that same day. Maybe not for a week. I've never come home with a baby before and I hate doing anything for the first time. Besides, I want to be ready when I go up. Ready for Kevin, but also for Cathy, who really will have a beef. I mean she's been living alone with Mama and Papa for three years now. It's not going to be easy for her—my moving in with a baby. But I want to get ready for everybody's reaction, even Mama and Papa's. There are bound to be rough spots, and I'm counting on you to help me get over them.

So whatever you do, don't tell anyone in the family what ship I'm taking or when I'm arriving. You're the only two I want to see at first. We can go somewhere, maybe to your place, and talk. God— New York! I never love it so much as in the autumn.

The new fall clothes, the new plays, the fresh energy, and the McIntosh apples—I can hardly wait!

Listen, I'm making Maderini a very special dinner (it takes three days just to prepare it) so I have to go.

Love,
OONA O'

CHAPTER XIII

The *Vulcania* slid upriver abreast of her berth on West 44th Street and reversed engines, lost headway, went astern a bit, stopped. Then, so slowly that at any given moment she appeared stationary in the water, she made a sweeping turn shoreward.

Jim and Nancy, as far out over the water as the upper level of the pier allowed, watched the whole operation in a wind rich with the smell of fuel oil, gasoline, factories, graphite, carbon, hay, rubber, garbage, and soot—all of it mixed in with, encompassed by, the marvelous, cosmopolitan tang of the river and the sea. They heard the signaling toots from ship to tugs and watched as the tugs, pushing against the ship's flanks, brought the bow around. New Yorkers, they had seen it all before, but now it was as if the spurts of steam from the ship and the kick of water behind the tugs and the megaphone shouts and the scurrying of sailors on deck had something definite, something decisive, to do with Oona. The tugboat men and the Italian captain and the officers and crew were all very responsible seamen. The care they were taking to get Oona and her baby ashore was enormous. Other passengers

were involved, tons of cargo were involved, reputa-
tions and jobs were involved, but someone they
knew was on the ship, and so everybody connected
with the operation was simply marvelous—just what
the world needed at a time like this.

Hawsers as thick as a man's calf and as long as a
city block were pulled and tugged by dockmen
through the slickly black water and looped around
bollards. Like a floating city, her tautened lines
dripping with tension, the ship edged closer. But no
sign of Oona among the hundreds searching for, or
waving to, friends on the pier. No sign of anyone
with a child.

They went to the middle of the pier where the
crowd stood waiting for the gangplank to be rigged.
Silent, apprehensive, they weren't ready to join the
hubbub yet. Oona might not even be aboard. It
would be just like her to miss a ship, the slowest and
most patient of vehicles, and miss it for the un-
likeliest reasons. Maderini's car broke down on the
way to Genoa. He fixed it, but in doing so broke the
nosepiece to his glasses. By the time he had the
nosepiece fixed (with Scotch tape that Oona had
had to open all her luggage to find), they found
themselves surrounded by cows. After getting past
the cows, they sped along until they entered a
falling-rock area that really was a falling-rock area:
boulders all over the road. Even so, and even
counting the amputation that Maderini had had to

perform on the farmer caught in the teeth of his own tractor, they still would have made it if not for that total eclipse of the sun they'd run into in that little mountain town. Farmers all over the road, holding their children up on their shoulders and passing the isinglass around. Couldn't make any time at all. They reached the pier minutes late, seconds late, but late.

When *Vulcania* passengers finally began pouring off, Jim and Nancy, really anxious now, got as close as possible to the actual point of contact between gangplank and pier. Extra precautions. With Oona you had to take them. Otherwise, even if she was on the ship, you'd lose her, or she'd lose you. She had a way of appearing, of looking all over for you, and then of disappearing just when your back was turned. So you never could have your back turned. You had to look, and look, and look. It was really a terrible nuisance.

Suddenly they saw her, or someone who resembled her, someone, anyway, with an infant, and shouted up, "Oona!"

She saw them and waved, waved frantically, wildly, joyously—it was Oona all right—and started down. Only, as she drew closer, she resembled herself less and less, less than she had from a distance. The writer of those letters couldn't be this weak and painfully thin girl whose long legs, on top of the inevitable *high* high heels, looked like toothpicks under the hem of her dress. And yet there were those ridiculously green, those startled and startling, eyes, smiling at them as though she'd finally found the solution to everything. Wait till you hear this! her smile seemed to say, so filled was it with hope and desire and the belief that good things were still somehow possible.

"Well," she said, both feet on the pier at last, "*well!* What do you think?"

She was referring, of course, to Sheila, as fat, healthy and self-satisfied in her cocoon of security as any mother or father could have wished.

"Oh, she's beautiful!" Nancy said. But the tears in her eyes were for Oona, whom she knew, not for the baby, whom she didn't know—for Oona who looked ten years older. Putting her arms around both of them, mother and child, she wet Oona's cheek with her tears as they kissed.

"God, you Italians," Oona said. "Give you eyes to cry with, I swear, and you'll never need a diuretic." She was crying herself, but she was Irish so it didn't count.

"What a baby!" Jim said, though his face too was caught in pain. Oona didn't even seem to know how terrible she looked. Day by day the mirror must have ushered her past the crisis without even telling her there was one. She had seen only her thriving baby, Sheila O', seen only her baby's growth, never her own deterioration.

Shipboard acquaintances, meanwhile, were tossing Oona their last goodbyes. "Don't forget, Oona, you said you'd call." "Don't *you* forget." "I won't." "All right, then. Bye." "Bye, now . . ." And another: "I meant that last night, Oona. I really did. Between Christmas and New Year's. All right?" "Bye, then. See you. Bye."—all with smiles that nullified the words themselves.

Then the festivities ended, the crowd thinned, and they were left backstage—with foremen, longshoremen, inspectors, sailors.

"What about your luggage?" Nancy said after Oona had gone through customs. "We have the car."

"It's being dropped off at your apartment."

"Oh."

"A friend—all right?"

"Of course!"

They had to move out of the way as a contraption of some kind, on wheels, approached. After it passed, Oona waited ten, fifteen seconds, no more. Then she said, "All right, out with it. What's the matter? Are you glad, or sorry, to see me?"

"You've lost so much weight, Oona, that's all," Jim said. "Haven't you been eating?"

"On the way over, just on the way over, I gained five pounds."

"What'd they do, bring you aboard on a stretcher?"

"No, in a cargo net. They ran out of stretchers."

This was what she wanted, though, the open expression of their concern, not the mopey concealment of it. With a joke thrown in, that is, a laugh attached. Nancy looked at them and was amazed for perhaps the thousandth time at the quickness of their response to the power of words. Give the Irish a twist of wit and immediately the blood begins to flow. They become lambs. Nothing wrong with the world. Poverty? Sickness? Pain? Bah!

"Here, let me carry her," Jim said.

"About *time*," Oona said, and with seeming carelessness, the inalienable aplomb of motherhood, handed the baby over.

Though not yet a father himself, Jim felt the same provisional joy, the same tenderness mingled with love and awe, that a father feels on holding his first-born. He was astonished not so much by the baby's *being* in his arms as by the emotions thereby set in motion in his heart. Every father is surprised at how great is his capacity to love his child, and it was this, the unexpected power of the emotion, the difference between the emotion itself and what had been anticipated, that struck Jim with such force. Too close in age to Oona and Cathy to have had any family experience with infants, he was being drawn for the first time into that world where the adult loses himself in the existence not of a wife or friend but of a completely dependent, an almost *incipient*, human being. Indeed it was this *dependence* on the part of Sheila, her seeming willingness to be carried, dropped, put in an ashcan, or taken home, that turned Jim into a stereotype of the anxious father before they had even reached the Twelfth Avenue end of the pier. On the cobblestones themselves, a jaywalker all his life, he became militantly aware of every passing cab and truck, he looked north and south, squared his jaw, strangled the loose edges of the baby's blanket.

"It's good I didn't wrap her in the Stars and Stripes," Oona said, noticing the spectacle he was making of himself.

"Why, what do you mean?"

"You're not crossing the *Delaware*."

"No, I'm crossing Twelfth, which is much worse."

"Take the baby, Nancy, will you? We look too much like a kidnap ring this way."

At the car, as Jim handed the baby to Nancy, he said in an undertone, so Oona wouldn't hear, "Stop it, Nancy. *Stop* it."

Rejecting the undertone, in fact, *raising* her voice, Nancy said, "Stop *what*?"

"Stop it, that's all. The long face, the *crying*, God damn it."

"Listen," Nancy said, and because she so seldom lost her temper, they both immediately gave her their attention, "I'm not you, her brother. I'm her friend. I don't care what *you* do. How *you* act. But don't you dare tell *me* how to act."

"Please, wait a minute," Oona said. "I'm here. I'm back. Really. And the thing is—"

"I'm not Oona either," Nancy went on. "I'm not Irish. All concentrated in my talking box the way you two are. The larynx, that Irish organ where words are born, Irish words, lovely words, lying words."

For a moment it was not at his wife that Jim stared but at Oona's best friend, that lovely mystery who had still not decided to marry him. When, almost immediately, she became his wife again, the mystery deepened, grew even lovelier, by assuming his name. Of all women in the world, this unquestionably was the one he knew best. Was she his wife? Did he know her at all? What in God's name did she mean by the larynx being an "Irish organ"?

"Go ahead, then," he said. "Cry. Cry down in the recesses, the cavities. Down in the visceral organs where Italians are concentrated. Is that where they're concentrated? And besides, since when are the recesses the only places? The larynx may not be all tunneled *in*, it may be closer to the surface than the Italian organs, but at least it gets an airing once in a while, a little fresh air."

"I hate you," Nancy said. "I hate you *and* your larynx."

"No, really, I'm here," Oona said. "And what I wish you'd give some consideration to—like in Florence, when I went to the Consulate the last time. You remember what I said in my letter? I'll bet you don't."

"What does the Consulate have to do with it?"

"Jim, the analogy is so obvious, you could almost touch it with your nose. Inch forward a little, Jim. Shoulders back, chin in, eyes straight ahead—forward *harch!*"

"Listen, Oona, ever since you were able to talk, you've done this. I've listened to you, I've studied all those ridiculous facial expressions of yours, I've concentrated. And for what? What have you ever said? I mean really said. What? Tell me. And what are you saying now?"

Just the same, it was refreshing to switch the attack from wife to sister. One soldier shouts to another, Who goes there, friend or enemy? And the other soldier shouts back, Who knows? They've just switched sides again.

"You finished, Jim? I said I felt like an object at the Consulate. Remember? Well, you and Nancy arguing. Same thing. I'm the subject of your argument, but the more you argue, the more incidental to the argument I feel. *I* don't count. Argument counts. Get it now? Subject . . . object." She gave them a schoolmarmish smile, a really wild one, as much as to say, If two plus two equals four, then four plus four equals . . . two plus two, *plus* two plus two, right? "Maybe you should both join the foreign service. You ever think of that?"

Familiar with her capricious way of thinking, and aware that she was really just trying to break up the argument, they were both nevertheless touched by her "analogy." They *were* thinking more of themselves than they were of her, *were* vying with each other for the "prize" of loving her the most, the deepest, the longest, the strongest.

Inside the car, with Jim behind the wheel, the two girls in the back, and Sheila on Nancy's lap, they fell silent again while Jim searched for his keys. He couldn't find them, and still no one spoke.

Of course, Oona thought. In America *no* one speaks until the motor turns over. Motor's everything. Jim knows it, Nancy knows it, I know it. We're not kidding ourselves. All the visceral *organs* are in the motor. Plymouth with Italian parts. She smiled: Where'd he dig that one up? Columbia? No wonder they lost so many games.

So while Jim fumbled for his keys, the motor *became* everything in Oona's mind. It became the reason for their friendship, Lincoln's Gettysburg Address, Boulder Dam, W. C. Fields, the Securities and Exchange Commission, and the drummer at Radio City Music Hall. A motor. God, without one what good would *anything* be? The Russians could have the place. She, for one, wouldn't fight.

Suddenly, and without a hitch, the motor started, and it was true, their *own* pistons and pumps began working again. Jim swung into 44th Street and you could see the leverage and sway of his shoulders as he turned the wheel to avoid holes in the pavement. Nancy, "alone" with Sheila at last, nuzzled down into the blanket to look at her, to kiss her, to pull the sweetness of her up into her nostrils. Oona leaned back and tried to relax, to get used to her city again. She remembered the old, wonderful, happy days of fraternity dances, the Lion's Den and week-end dates—the chrysanthemum Saturdays up at Baker Field when Jim, one of Lou Little's "sixty-minute men," was always the muddiest and sweatiest player on the field. Very softly, she began singing: "Oh, who owns New *York?* Oh, who owns New *York?* Oh, who owns New *York*—the people say—" Suddenly she leaned forward. "Oh, listen! You know who I saw in Genoa just before I left? Irene McLaughlin. Remember her, Nancy? Girl from Morningside Drive when Morningside was where we *all* wanted to live?"

"She still swing her left arm that same way when she walks? With the little wrist movement at the end?"

"The end of the backward swing, you mean, right? As though she were patting her behind each time? Nancy, how'd you ever *remember* that? You even have the arm right."

"You *forgot* that about Irene? How about how we used to duck into vestibules and behind cars whenever we saw her coming?"

"That I remembered. In fact, when I saw her coming toward me in Genoa, it was like living through one of her endless stories all over again. What her uncle said, and what her father said back, and how her aunt disagreed with both of them. God, that family of hers, relatives visiting back and forth month after month and year after year. I swear, I'd rather spend the rest of my life blowing bubbles than be stuck in a family like that. I mean who *cares* which uncle said what to which aunt? But Irene had to clear it up, she had to get it straight in your mind before she'd even tell you what the uncle said. I admit she created a little suspense that way, but it only added to the letdown afterward. Because what her uncle said you could hear on the subway anytime. Rush hour especially. I mean it. A child from a family like that is doomed from the start, because here are these grown-ups, you see, and what they do, they spend all their waking hours, their lives, practically, deciding questions like who carved the turkey after So-and-So's wedding twenty years before. Poor Irene . . ."

"Well, come on!" Nancy said. "Was she with her mother? She married? You spend much time with her?"

"Right there, Nancy. Stop right there. That's the whole point, what I'm coming to. I mean there we were, three thousand miles from home, two girls from the same neighborhood, approaching each other in a foreign city—and what do I do? Snap your fingers. That's how long it takes me to duck into a doorway."

"With the baby and all?"

"No. Baby's already aboard, in the ship's nursery, but Maderini's with me and that's where the fun comes in—his face as I grab his arm and say, 'In here, Elio. Quick!' Could've been an air raid, the way he hops right in with me. Hallway of some kind, dark, and we can hardly see. I open my eyes wide, but he's really in the dark, you know? So his are bulging. 'What is it, Oona?' he says. 'Are you ill?'

" 'Not so loud!' I tell him. 'Girl coming this way. American with straw hat. Tall, yellow dress. Sharp, narrow face. Freckles.'

" 'No escort?' he says.

" 'That's the one,' I tell him, and that's all. We wait there and Irene passes, the sun on her dress. Few more seconds and we're walking along again, only Maderini can't stop turning around. Can't take his eyes off Irene, who's really stepping along, patting her behind to beat the band. Let's face it, Nancy, it is an interesting walk. Anyway, Maderini finally turns to me and says, 'Well, what else?'

" 'I know her from New York, that's what else,' I tell him. 'And that's all the what else I need. Grew up with her. Same neighborhood. Same school. Same age. Everything.'

" 'That is all?' he says. 'You know her? Therefore we must hide?'

" 'No one ever hides in Italy, I suppose,' I tell him.

" 'Oona,' he says, 'I try to understand you. I try hard. Believe me. But you do not help me to understand. For example, is there something . . . political?'

" 'There's Italy for you,' I tell him. 'I duck into a doorway for political reasons and it's all right. Is that it? No explanation necessary. Well, I'm sorry, Elio, I just know the girl, that's all.'

" 'And in America,' he says, 'I must hide also, if I see a man from Fiesole?'

" 'In America,' I tell him, 'you feel like hiding, you hide. Nobody's going around telling you to hide.'

"He looks around once more and I know it's to see if Irene's still patting her behind. Tell you the truth, he's beginning to act as if *he's* in a foreign country. Anyway, Irene's disappeared. We're walking along again and he says, 'One thing I know for sure. Before, I am not so sure. Now I am very sure. I will never go to America.' "

"What a distorted picture that poor guy must

have of this country," Jim said. "Hanging around with you. Why didn't you just tell him about Irene?"

"He can't take his eyes off her and I'm supposed to tell him she's a bore? Listen, if anybody doesn't look like a bore, it's Irene McLaughlin walking. And when she's in a hurry it's even worse. I swear, *everybody* was looking at her, and if some Italian hasn't raped her by now, there'll be only one reason for it. She started telling him about her family. Besides, I finally *did* tell Maderini what she was. I came right out with it and said she was a hopeless bore. And you know what that chauvinist said? 'They are here also. You think only America has them?'

"We're on our way to the ship, and we're fooling around, arguing back and forth like that, right up to the last minute. Then I just *have* to get aboard, so we embrace each other, and you should see him. The tears are *rolling* down his cheeks. I'm crying too, of course, but I'm a piker next to him. I mean Italians know *how* to cry. They also know *when*, and how long to keep it up. We never *did* get to say goodbye because of him. We just didn't say it, we were too busy crying. We waved to each other, as the ship pulled out. But the way we were waving, the ship might have been pulling in. All I know is, we never did actually say goodbye."

A reflective little gap followed, then, at a red light

Jim said, "Be great to go to a bar now, wouldn't it?"

"With the baby we can't, you mean," Oona said. "No, of course not. Would be great, though. Really would."

"How about if I leave Sheila at Bellevue for a while?" Jim said. "With a nurse. Nothing to worry about. We have dinner somewhere. Three, four hours, we go back and get her."

"We haven't been to the Cave Inn for years," Nancy said.

"The Cave Inn. Great!" Oona glanced at her watch. "Off-hour, too. Best time."

At the hospital, as they entered "Staff Only" to park, Oona slipped her hand under the blanket and took hold of her daughter's feet. "Sheila takes size one, Jim. They have straight-jackets that small?"

"There's nothing to *worry* about, Oona." He parked and got out and went around and took the baby from Nancy. "Better if I go in myself. So you two take a cab and I'll see you there in fifteen minutes." As he walked away he called back. "She'll be fine here, Oona. So go ahead. I'll be there—most a half hour."

CHAPTER XIV

The Cave Inn was a dark woody place close enough to Grand Central and generous enough with liquor to make it a favorite among the Connecticut editors, writers and cartoonists who on weekdays invaded New York. From twelve to two and from five to six it was three deep at the bar: well-dressed men with a light salting of interesting and courageous women of the type men don't mind having around but hardly ever, out of an instinct for dominance or survival or both, marry. This was the off-hour, though, so Oona and Nancy went to their favorite spot at the end of the bar, the end nearest the tree outside (how it had grown!), where there happened to be three unoccupied stools.

"You still martini, Oona?"

"With water on the side. Maderini's orders."

Nancy threw her coat over the outside stool to reserve it for Jim—"Order me one"—and went to the ladies' room.

When the drinks came, in glasses whose frostiness told Oona she was no longer in Florence, she looked at hers, took a sip, found the necessary correspondence between its appearance and taste, and placed it carefully back down on the bar. Then as though suddenly remembering another way to be nice to herself, she opened her bag and began to freshen up.

Besides being a very light drinker, with a taste, an actual *taste*, for martinis, Oona was the last person anyone would expect to see sitting at a bar alone. Nancy would soon be back and Jim was coming, of course, but even so, Oona looked too much like some college president's daughter to be right up there with the drinkers. Oona loved it, though, the way it *was* in New York bars, especially during the off-hours when the pros were there, the men who sat silently waiting for their potions to be brought to them. They'd see her come in and know she was there for a potion herself, and it helped them, she could tell it did. They wouldn't say anything to her or bother her in any way, but every now and then, very *cas*ually, and with a patience, a finesse, not to be found on the subway, they'd look over at her and she'd look over at them. The difference was that in a bar you were in the thing together, in the same pew, so to speak, having your potions brought to you and all. You were admitting you weren't perfect. You needed the potion, and you wanted people around while you were having it. And though Oona didn't need it, she really didn't, she could see where she might someday, when she was older and maybe still unmarried and Sheila was up at Smith skiing with some Dartmouth boy and all. Something personal like that seemed to have happened to the men in bars, the pros especially, and if her walking in helped them—well, fine.

After pressing the excess lipstick off on her napkin, she took another sip and edged her stool closer to the wall to get more of a corner angle on things. From now on, everyone who stepped in for a drink would be a "walk-on." She was already there on her stool, she had already sipped her drink, and so she and the others on stools were the audience. A walk-on would qualify as part of the audience only when he or she ordered a drink and took a sip.

"You all fixed, miss?" the bartender said. It was the nightman, newly arrived, his first drink of the day still unmade—a walk-on himself. "Yes. I see you are. Good—fine." Hands on hips, hands at sides, hands running back and forth over the bar, the man seemed extremely ill at ease about something. The dayman, maybe that was it. Yes, that was it. The dayman hadn't left yet, he was still behind the bar, so the nightman was strictly neither-nor. Why didn't the dayman finish up and leave, instead of counting his tips like that?

By the time Nancy rejoined her, the nightman had the bar to himself. And what a difference!

"Look at him, Nancy. He's wonderful."

"Who?"

"New bartender just came on. I knew he didn't

feel right with the dayman here. All right, dayman's gone and now look at him. Boy, is he taking over."

The nightman had not so much as touched a glass, rag or napkin with the dayman present. Now, with an intensity out of all proportion to what he was actually doing, he was changing the position of every single bottle behind the bar. This was another thing about a bar during the off-hours: the bartender's methods took on such tremendous importance. Without a word, Nancy and Oona edged over to get a better look at the labels. They wanted to know why he was rearranging the bottles, what made him alternate two whiskey bottles, say, or move a certain brand of gin from the lower to the upper shelf. The grouping wasn't alphabetical, it had nothing to do with the proof, color, or kind of liquor in each bottle, or even with how much was left in a bottle.

"Ask him, Oona, will you? I can't stand it any more."

"You know what I think?" Oona said. "It has no meaning."

"Don't be silly. Look at him. He's much too exact for it to have no meaning."

"Wait. I think I've got it. It's a formula."

"What kind of formula?"

"Formula to rid the place of the dayman. That's why we couldn't figure it out. It's a private formula.

Only he knows it."

"Ask him, will you, Oona?" Even as she said it, she realized that she had become as involved in the thing as Oona, and she recalled Maderini's "When I am with her, she makes me not worry." It was true, Oona didn't even look sick any more. She was thinner, yes, much thinner, but Nancy was already used to that. The thinness went with Oona now. There was color in Oona's face, a crazy delight in her eyes. And all because a bartender was changing bottles behind a bar. It was dangerous just being with her, so quickly did she make you forget she was sick.

The bartender, having rearranged the bottles to his satisfaction, came over with a smile and asked the girls if they wanted another.

"Yes, please," Oona said. "And listen, would you do us a favor? My friend here is making a survey."

"She is?" He looked happy as hell now that his bottles were in order. "What kind of survey?"

"Oh, one of those NAM things for the Voice of America broadcasts. Maybe you've heard of it. 'Life Behind the American Bar. Facts and figures on the habits and attitudes of American bartenders.' Anyway, what Nancy here would like to know—and your name'll be withheld if you want it withheld—is why did you do that to the bottles when you came on duty?"

The man put both forearms on the bar in a way

that the Chief Justice of the Supreme Court could not have improved upon. "I've been asked that one before."

"You have?"

"Many times. And the answer's always the same. To get them in order."

"But what kind of order? They seemed to be in pretty good order when you came on duty."

"They were in order. I'm not knocking the other man. I've worked with him for years and I know he can't help it. The trade, you see, is different early in the day."

"The trade?" Oona said, with such emphasis, such urgent concern, that the man automatically hunched over in a position more appropriate to the exchanging of confidences. Oona did not tear down social barriers so much as prevent them from ever going up.

"Man in the back," the bartender whispered out of the side of his mouth. "Reading *World-Telegram*. One of my steadies, Old-Crow-on-the-rocks man. Comes in every day without fail. Exact same time. Exact same drink. All right? Now, let's say he did come in early in the day when I wasn't here. Don't think he would, but let's say he did. He wouldn't order Old-Crow-on-the-rocks, would he, that early in the day? He might, but chances are he'd order a more liquidy drink. Vitamin C. Bloody Mary, whiskey sour, beer. Because drinkers are always thirsty in the morning, you see? So the other bartender—don't get me wrong—he doesn't mean to change my setup, but he does, he can't help it, with the trade he's got."

"So your arrangement is based on the trade you get in the evening?"

"Exactly. I know where my steadies are, you see, and what drinks they're going to order. I also know what drinks the transients order from four o'clock on when they have maybe fifteen minutes, half hour, before train time. So wherever I am in this bar—here, in the back, over at the service counter—I got my bottles handy."

"You know," Oona said, "I can tell just from looking at Nancy. All her life she's wanted to be an aviatrix, but now she's going to be a bartender."

"Not in New York she isn't. The union doesn't allow it." He became Chief Justice again. "You'll have to go out of state, Nancy."

"I'll go out of state, then," Nancy said. "I'll go anywhere."

The man picked up their glasses and, for someone so big and hefty, clinked them very daintily. "Not supposed to, but you girls—crazy. So this one's on me."

By the time Jim arrived, the place was as crowded as the 5:10 train to Westport, so the three of them locked themselves in the corner, street window on their right, tight-skinned men from Connecticut on their left. They continued fooling around, but the conversation inevitably turned to Oona's parents and it was Jim's idea that she should see them while she was still thin.

"You go up tomorrow or the next day, Oona. They see you. They look at you, and they're so sympathetic that nobody *else* says a word. Even Kevin shuts up. Meanwhile, you're *there*, and everybody's getting used to your being there. Mama's fattening you up. She's making all your favorite dishes. Tripe in cream sauce . . ."

"That's Papa's favorite dish. Mine's crabmeat au gratin, and Mama hates grating the Parmesan."

"You can buy it already grated."

"That's been one of the sore points between Mama and me for years. Nancy, am I right? Is that *sand* you get in a jar any good?" (Nancy shook her head.) "I *knew* it."

"Now *wait* a minute," Nancy said. "Don't tell your *mother* I said that. You hear, Oona? I don't want to be brought into any argument between you and your mother about *cheese*."

"You afraid of my mother?"

"You heard me, Oona. Don't laugh. I *mean* it."

"I try to talk to you two, I swear," Jim said, "and I get this feeling I'm turning into cereal."

"If it isn't Ralston's, we don't want it . . ."

And so it went, on and on. Oona refused to be

maneuvered into a position where she would evoke sympathy from her family. Could she and Sheila stay at Jim and Nancy's for a few days until she got used to being back? She'd have a great meal for them when they came home in the evening. They could have drinks, eat, get Sheila to sleep and talk.

"It's a bargain," Jim said. "If you let me take you to a doctor."

"A doctor? I just left a doctor."

"In Italy you left him. He's not here, is he? I want you to have a complete physical checkup, Oona. I'll take you myself, to a specialist, and it won't cost you a nickel. Is it a bargain?"

"Not tomorrow, though. And probably not the next day either."

"But soon. You hear? I'm not fooling. Soon."

CHAPTER XV

Oona stayed at Jim and Nancy's a week and gained four more pounds before calling home to say she had just arrived. A lie, but she needed the extra time to prepare for her mother, who would naturally expect to be trifled with rather than depended upon.

"Just arrived, Ma. By plane. That's right. Still at Idlewild, in fact. So listen, will you? For once? You heard me. For once. I only want to see you and Papa and Cathy when I get there. All right? No, nothing's wrong, Ma. I just don't want any big family pow-wow, that's all." She was calling from Jim and Nancy's, who were out.

"All right, Oona, all right." With unhurried grace and smooth water all around it, a freighter slid into view on its way down the Hudson. Loaded, Maggie noticed, the crew battening down hatches and lowering booms. "You come back from Europe and what do you do? Shout at your mother. Can't wait." She went on in this vein but kept looking at the freighter too, even going so far as to change her position at the window in order to follow it with her eyes downstream. Then without effort, perhaps for

no other reason than that the freighter was leaving
New York instead of, like Oona, coming into New
York, she got the feeling that something was out of
true and not to be depended upon. "What about
Jim and Nancy?" she said.

"They may come up with me."

"You've seen them already? I knew it. Just arrived at Idlewild but you've seen Jim and Nancy already. What'd you do, pick them up in Newfound-
land?"

Oona smiled. Well, this was why she had waited
a week. With her mother you had to be in cham-
pionship condition. "I haven't seen them, Ma.
They're still coming. I'm waiting for them. I called
and asked them to help me with my luggage, that's
all. In fact I distinctly remember saying to myself as
I dialed their number, If only Mama were still a
cabby, I'd call her instead."

"Wait'll you get here. I'll show you who the
cabby is. I'll show you a few other things too. I
mean it, Oona, I do. You're really going to get it this
time."

"In Samoa I wouldn't have to take this."
"Where?"

"Samoa. Land of the banana leaf and the butterfly god. You'd be tabooed in Samoa, Ma. No, it used
to be where you were only tabooed. Now they tattoo
you first and then taboo you. The other change is it
takes three days now, whereas before the children's

referendum it only took a day. Then on the fourth day, as the rising sun lights up the butterfly flag they always use when they taboo a mother who's been mean to her child—and this part they haven't changed—they send you away on the one-eyed elephant."

"Oona, what's wrong with you? Sometimes I really think there *is* something." Maggie would never have admitted it, but she loved Oona to "go to work" on her this way. It made her feel more like a girl friend and put her more in touch with the springs of life, the young ones, her own children and still growing grandchildren, who were pushing her out of the world but not because they wanted to, they just were. Right now, though, she mustn't let on, because part of Oona's game was that you weren't supposed to say it was a game or even act as though it were a game. You could resist being sent away on the one-eyed elephant, you could even doubt the elephant's existence. Oona had no objection to that so long as you kept a straight face. Otherwise all bets were off.

"You're a mother now yourself, Oona. Remember that. Just remember it. Because if anybody's going to ride that one-eyed elephant, you are . . ." The freighter had passed, and now, down below in the park across the street, children were running from a birdbath with loaded water pistols, Columbia University couples were strolling by hand in hand, a bus was roaring north on its way to Fort Tryon. Already, it seemed, she had relinquished herself to the benign indifference of the neighborhood where, on summer evenings as a girl (was it fifty years ago?), she had walked through open fields filled with squatters' goats to watch the splendid couples dancing under lanterns at the Claremont Inn. Pushed out of the world. All right, then let Oona do the pushing. That way she wouldn't know she was gone until after she'd left. Painless— "Is Sheila all right?" she went on. "That *is* her name, isn't it? Sheila?"

"Yes, and she's fine, Ma. A real doll. I mean a *real* doll."

"Oona, the way you say that—"

"Ma, stop saying 'the way you say that,' will you? You're *always* saying it, and not only to me, either. You say it to everybody."

"It better not be a real doll, Oona, that's all. I mean it. If it isn't a real baby, I'm serious, I'll never forgive you."

Oona couldn't resist. "You want it to be a baby that much?"

"I've been led to *believe* it's a baby. How would *you* like to be told—and then—"

"All right, Ma, all *right!* I'll see what I can do."

"What do you *mean*, you'll see what you can do?"

"I mean with the population explosion and all, it

shouldn't be too difficult. So on the way up I'll see what I can do."

"Oona, please!"

"Okay, Ma. Calm down, will you? Of course it's a real baby. Why didn't you write me a *letter* like this when I was in Italy, though? What a difference it would have made."

"Did you have trouble in Italy, Oona?"

"You talking about the border incident? Or the one in the interior?"

"Be serious. When are you getting here? I want to look at you."

"Between three and four, on that one condition, though, you hear? No family powwow. Just you and Papa and Cathy at first. The others gradually, one at a time, with plenty of space in between. You asked me to be serious, Ma. All right, I'm serious. I'll be there this afternoon."

"You taking a cab up, or is Jim driving you?"

"What's the difference?"

"Supper. That's the difference. If Jim and Nancy are coming, I'll get a whole salmon. Otherwise salmon steaks."

"Friday, that's right. Well, get the whole salmon, then, Ma. Papa and I like it better creamed the next day anyway, if Jim and Nancy don't come."

"I'll start with creamed salmon, then, all right? With plenty of parsley in the sauce. You love that."

"Will you shut up about the salmon, Ma?"

"All right, Oona. Between three and four, then. Your father and I will be here."

She hung up and called the fish store. Five pounds of salmon. "Yes, Joe, I'm creaming it, so the tail ends'll be fine. Better even."

Hanging up again she realized for the first time that her heart was pounding. Oona with a baby? A baby girl? *Oona?* She tried to conjure up some kind of image of Oona's child, but it was too much like an Our Gang Comedy with "Sheila" playing all the roles. The sensational remark, yes. The extravagant action, yes. The bizarre thought, yes. She could see those coming from Oona. But a real child? No, she'd have to see this Sheila first, which was what she *wanted* to do, why her heart was pounding so.

Her husband walked in while she was still on the phone sharing the news with other members of the family. He caught the gist of it and was struck by how the excitement, the telephoning, made him think Oona was going to need help. Between calls, when Maggie told him the details, he suggested she skip Kevin.

"Friday's his busy day and I'll be seeing him on Monday anyway. Besides, Kevin doesn't exactly see eye to eye with Oona. *You* know that."

"I don't care. She's coming from Europe with a baby and he's her brother."

"And you're their *mother*. I know. So go ahead,

call him. Only leave me out of it. I come home and you tell me Oona'll be here this afternoon. No family powwow, you tell me she says . . ." It embarrassed him to say "powwow," but what better proof was there that Oona was back than something like that passing his lips? Like her teaching him the rumba last Thanksgiving. Embarrassing as *hell*, until he had begun to get the hang of it, and then he had felt, well, *what* the hell.

"I'm not inviting the others," Maggie said. "I'm just telling them."

"They drop around on their own. You going to tell them they can't come in?"

"You make me think something's wrong, John. Did you have words with Kevin about Oona?"

"No! And there's nothing wrong, Maggie. Will you get that idea out of your head? Oona said no powwow, that's all."

"Will you stop saying that, John? You're as bad as she is. She probably gets it from you."

"What—powwow?"

"There you go again."

"Maggie, I've never in my life—"

"Not that exactly. The whole idea. Like when she was a child, the stories you used to tell her."

"I told the same stories to everybody. Made them up as I went along."

"Why did you always make up better ones when she was listening? Tell me that."

"Could I help it if she *took* to them more than the others did? That face of hers—you *had* to be good."

"You *were* good, John. 'Land of the butterfly god.' You were very good."

"What in God's name are you talking about? Did you ever, in your life, hear me say that? Now Maggie, did you?"

"You know what I mean. The thief of Bagdad and all. Did you ever tell a story that didn't have a flying carpet in it? Or a magic piece of rope?"

"My imagination doesn't *compare* with yours, Maggie, and 'butterfly god' proves it."

"So you don't want me to call Kevin?"

"Do what you want."

"I won't call him, then. You can tell him on Monday."

"You want me to vacuum?"

"Perry's coming to do the windows. He can vacuum. If you want to do something, why don't you go and get some liquor?" Like most people who run bars, John O'Hagen almost never had any liquor on hand at home.

"After I take a shower and get dressed. What's the baby's name again?"

"Sheila."

"That's right. Sheila Penhaligan. Nice name."

CHAPTER XVI

Oona stepped out of the car at her parents' address and for a moment it was as if the park across the street had its own idea of itself and that idea were entering her mind just as surely as her idea of it was forming. She stood there, her daughter in her arms, and took it in with her eyes and nose and, as the wind found her, her skin too. She had a wonderful love for that park: her childhood, youth, the games and sleigh rides and first boy kisses in the snow were all there hidden in the flickering tawny-green leaves like so many faces of herself that she had come back from Europe to find.

"Hundred and sixteenth and Riverside," she said. "Windiest corner in New York. I read it somewhere. Not that I had to. I *knew* it was."

"Go on up, Oona, stop stalling," Jim said. Family reunions bothered him, and this one, Oona back from Europe with a baby, well, he'd just as soon miss the first few minutes of it. "Go ahead. Nancy and I'll be getting the luggage."

"I'm trembling, though, Jim. I really am. Isn't that stupid? No fooling. I'm scared."

"*Don't* be. They're waiting for you. They *want* to
see you."

"Here goes, then."

She turned and entered the building's nave-like
stone entrance, once a sheltered driveway for Rolls
Royces, Pierce Arrows, La Salle roadsters and Cadillac touring cars. Now it was one of those West
Side reminders of the Twenties before the Crash:
Vitaphone and the Photoplay; "Seventh Heaven,"
"The Big Parade" and "Beau Geste"; cloche hats,
spats and plus-fours; Charles Lindbergh, Rudy
Vallee, Bill Tilden, Babe Ruth and Bobby Jones;
the Columbia football team playing on South Field
in front of Low Memorial Library, and Riverside
Drive as affluent and exclusive as the East Side was
now. She hadn't been born then. Her father had
told her about it and he knew because the owners of
the limousines, some of them Columbia Trustees,
had been his customers. And now her mother and
father lived here in this staunchly constructed building, old perhaps, but with twelve-foot-high ceilings,
two feet of concrete between floors, and enough
Italian marble in the lobby alone to line the walls of
Congress with.

The elevator. Thank goodness. No one. All the
way up without a stop, and Sheila dead to it all in
her arms. Would she come back to this moment
someday and say, yes, of course, I should have known
then what was going to happen? She felt loose,

uncertain; her emotions, inchoate and ungraspable, were forming a rich delta of possibilities up ahead.

When she found the front door ajar (was her mother watering the flower boxes on the roof?) she entered without knocking and walked through the foyer into what seemed an empty apartment. In the kitchen the window fan was going; there were dishes soaking in the sink; a chocolate layer cake had been partially eaten and put back under its plastic hood on top of the refrigerator. When, by force of habit, she opened the refrigerator and saw her mother's Frances Denny Skin Lotion standing in its usual place next to the freezing unit, the sense of familiarity and routine made her almost believe that since nothing had changed, nothing had happened. This minute, if she ran into the living room without thinking, without any design of any kind, she might still find the world of her childhood waiting for her. Sheila would be someone she'd found in the street (Could you use this baby, Ma?).

The "maid's" room off the kitchen, her father's room, might have been one of the pockets in her father's coat sweater. It had the same smell and was stuffed with the same kind of things: keys, tire gauges, baby screw-drivers, pencil stubs, toothpicks, and ancient cigarette butts that her father actually smoked now and then when he found that a pack was empty. Sometimes, in the sweater pockets themselves, the butts split from the weight of the keys, and then the tobacco spilled out and became part of the permanent stuffing in which all the other things were embedded.

She swung back into the kitchen, unnerved by the quiet of an apartment usually filled with vehement talk: Had her mother arranged some kind of surprise? Were the others, even Kevin, hiding? God!

"Mama?" she shouted. "Papa?"

"Who's that?" Maggie cried, and there was real fear, almost terror, in her voice. In the living room, she had the sofa away from the wall and was zipping up the slipcover she had just that week bought at Macy's. She had been saving it for Thanksgiving and then, after Oona's call, had decided, Well, use it.

"Who do you think?" Oona shouted back in an effort to be natural. (Why did her mother sound like that?) "I said between three and four, didn't I?"

Walking through the apartment as she spoke, she entered the living room just as Maggie, who for twenty-five years had not even walked fast, whose very grace now depended upon her setting her own pace, scrambled pathetically from behind the sofa, her face full of the same fear that had been in her voice, a fear that had nothing to do with Oona's appearance since Oona saw her first. It was the fear rather of an old woman's being taken by surprise, hopelessly caught, with more emotions than her aging heart could handle. She had known for hours that Oona was coming, and now, all because she'd been behind the sofa instead of sitting on it, she might as well have not known at all. The *slip-* cover was why she was breaking down, the *slip-* cover. No other reason.

"Why didn't you *tell* me you still had your key?" she cried, her tears blinding her, her arms reaching out for both of them, a single tear of Oona's like a blessing on her neck.

"I *don't* still have my key, Ma. The door was open."

"It *was?*" Maggie pounced on the door's complete irrelevance. "Your father! *He* left it open."

"All right, Ma. Stop it or I won't think you're glad to see me."

"See you—" Maggie stepped back. "Oona, what's—*happened* to you? You look—"

"Dropped a few pounds, Ma, that's all. Nothing to worry about." She stepped over and laid her daughter, still asleep, on the sofa and put a few throw pillows on the outside so Sheila wouldn't roll off, all the while painfully, *palpably* aware that she was being gone over from behind. Shoulder blades, vertebrae buttons, hip bones, that little thing at the *base* of the spine that always sticks out when you bend down if you're really thin—her whole damn *body* was being studied. "Sheila's a real baby, Ma, and you haven't said a word about her."

"I'll get to the baby," Maggie said. She had already dried her eyes, regained control of herself, forgotten all about herself. With Oona sick like this, really unwell, and here to be looked at, cared for, Maggie's confused emotions closed ranks and went on the march.

"Stop staring at me as though I didn't have a nose, Ma, will you? Ma, will you stop it?"

"How did you become pregnant?"

"I sat on a chair that some man had warmed."

"I mean if you were this sick, how did you? How did you carry the child?"

"We took turns. Part of the time I carried, part of the time the child carried."

"Oona—" She was crying again. "It isn't *funny!*"

But Oona couldn't help it. She hated all that First World War stuff where Marshall Foch pins the medal on you and even the real tough guys like Victor McLaglen and Louis Wolheim—your absolute pals even though they are only enlisted men—sniff and cry. Maybe she had just seen too many old movies at the Thalia, maybe that was it. What she really hated, though, was being made the object of pity or sorrow or even concern. I refuse to accept this assignment, she wanted to say to her mother. But there it was, in her mother's face, this very important assignment that had a deadline and everything.

"Oona, are you here?" It was her father, having just met Jim and Nancy on his way back from the liquor store, and now banging the bottles, almost breaking them, against the kitchen table.

"John? The living room," Maggie called. "Come in, my God, and look at her!"

"I'm leaving!" Oona said, and rushed over to get the baby. "I'm that much of a freak, you're going to have to pay admission."

John O'Hagen was positive—in court he would have sworn—that as he entered the living room his wife and daughter were wrestling!

"John, will you help me with this girl?" Maggie cried over her shoulder. "I can't look at her. I can't ask her how she got sick. If I don't joke about how she looks, she's going to leave."

"Stop it! Both of you!" O'Hagen shouted. "Five minutes—*two* minutes—and you're fighting already."

As Maggie let go, Oona turned and went to her father to be held—hidden from her mother—for a minute. He had just shaved, so she couldn't feel that bristly red beard which was so emphatically a part of her childhood, those days on his lap when she had found the hairs almost as good as owning a cat.

O'Hagen, as shocked and grieved by her appearance as his wife, was nevertheless able to appear more reasonable if only because Maggie had already done the spadework for him, the shock work. "*Are* you sick, Oona?" he said.

"*Is* she sick," cut in Maggie.

"Pa, will you tell that frustrated blood donor to stop it? I'm *not* sick. I *became* sick. I *was* sick. I'm no *longer* sick." Still holding on to him in a way that made him an ally whether or not he wanted to be, she swung on her mother. "The unforgivable sin is despair. Don't you *know* that?"

"John, I won't *have* her saying crazy things to me."

"Stop it, Oona, will you? *Both* of you stop it."

"What have *I* done?" Maggie said.

"Stop looking at her."

"I can't look at my own daughter?"

"Look at me when *I'm* not looking he means," Oona said. "Steal looks . . ."

"See what I mean, John?"

Suddenly Sheila saved the day with an outburst that very plainly said, What *is* this? Where *am* I?

John and Maggie both went to the baby and Maggie picked her up. Oona held back, waited, for despite the difficult birth, despite Mrs. Friedensohn's covetousness and all the American Consulate trouble, it was only now, now that her mother and father had her, that Sheila O' began really to exist. Oona's love for her parents had deepened rather than changed, her field of action had narrowed; out of necessity she had turned from the distractions of parties and the attentions of men rather than toward them. And now that she was home it was as if she had been intercepted and thrown backward in time, been made to relive her own childhood all over again.

Cathy came in with Jim and Nancy, who had asked her—quite naturally and innocently down in the building lobby—to help with Oona's luggage. Cathy of course helped, and though the chore took only a few minutes, it helped trigger the resentment she had unconsciously been building up toward Oona's return. Not counting Oona's trunk, there were seven bags in all. They were borrowed bags, old and new bags, different-shaped bags, some lead-heavy with books and some feather-light with Oona's crazy hats, and just helping to get them in and out of the elevator and into the apartment, just seeing them piled in the foyer, told Cathy how different her homelife was going to be from now on. Not that she disliked Oona—on the contrary, she found her fascinating and even tried to emulate her. But Oona had left home; she had gone out on her own, and when you did that, you were not supposed to come back.

To make matters worse, Cathy saw, on her way to the living room to greet Oona, the baby lying on the end of the sofa where the only good reading lamp

was, the end where she read the papers every night.
She knew the baby wasn't going to be kept permanently at that end of the sofa, but the sight of the
baby there suggested things about the future, just as
the sight of her father bending over and cooing to
the baby reminded her of what the older children in
the family used to say. "What happens to you, Pa,
every time a baby is born in this family? Are we
suddenly so complex by comparison that you can't
stand us any more?" It was true, the unformed
personality of the infant always seemed to shock
him into realizing how distinctly themselves the
others had become. Individuality in a child per-
plexed him in the same way that spoken English
would have in his canary, in part because he respected what he didn't own and wouldn't violate,
but also in part because he didn't know what to do
with so much individuality under one roof. Cathy,
at any rate, suddenly saw herself as one of the "older
children," saw Oona's baby as probably the last of
her father's unformed personalities, and it was on
this note, with her heart and mind confused, that
she went to Oona.

Oona extended her hand to her as much as to say,
Ever since I arrived I've been worrying about you
especially, what your reaction was going to be. They
embraced each other, and though Oona was still a
little taller, Cathy felt an almost boyish superiority.
Veins like pink filament showed through under

Oona's eyes; the eyes themselves had almost de-
voured the rest of her face; her forehead looked like
something you could poke your finger through.
Cathy noticed the looseness of Oona's shoulder
blades against the pressure of her hands and felt a
twinge of guilt at having hated to admit to herself in
the past that Oona was probably more beautiful
than she was.

"Thanks for writing all those letters, Cathy. They
must have been an awful nuisance," Oona said.

"Why didn't you come home, if you were sick
like this?" Cathy said. She had been swimming in
the school pool and she looked clean and fresh and
radiant; her rubbed skin glowed and her eyes,
flecked with red from the chlorine, sparkled like
sequins. She was tingling and crackling with life,
and Oona, away for six months, was enabled by distance to see her as being direct and honest in just
the right degree, in a way that made innocence the
least dispensable virtue in life.

"Don't you start," Oona said, warming to the
possibility of their becoming good friends as Cathy
went over to look at the baby. She glanced down at
Cathy's sleek tan legs and wondered if her legs
would ever look like that again, if she would ever be
really well again. Why did she realize she was sick
now that she was home? Was it because she could
afford to be sick now? Oh, stop it, she thought, and
said aloud, "Pa, how about a drink?"

"Jim, you make them, will you?" John O'Hagen said. "And, Nancy, you sit here, by me. I haven't seen you in what—three weeks?"

Talk, laughter, then more of the same. So no one paid much attention when Cathy left the room to answer the doorbell.

It was Kevin, standing in the hallway with one glove removed, the other glove in the process of being removed. Watch closely, ladies and gentlemen, he seemed to be saying, and you will see my fingers appear one at a time. Kevin loved gloves and wore them nine months of the year. In fact, he had a glove collection, and at Christmas the trick was to "surprise" him by giving him gloves in shirt, underwear, and bedroom-slipper boxes. One Christmas Oona used a falsely weighted Lionel train box, but since he found gloves rather than trains inside, the Christmas amenities were preserved. Then when everybody grew up and stopped exchanging presents, even that small tribute to family affection and the meaning of Christmas came to an end, and with it the once-a-year truce it imposed on Kevin and Oona.

"Oh, it's you," Cathy said, and opened the door wide for him to enter.

He gave her a nod, his only concession to her existence except for holy days of obligation, and stepped in. But suddenly, seeing the foyer in as many new lights as there were handbags in it, he stopped and with great suspicion (Where were you on the night of—) turned back to her. For the voice, the words, reaching him from the living room, could only be Oona's.

"In Italy just before I left," Oona was saying, "I was talking to this American girl who said she was seriously thinking of getting a divorce—for three hundred dollars, she said—because her husband had asked her to lend him fifty dollars until he got his commission with the occupying forces over there. I asked her, 'Is it worth three hundred?' and she said, 'Well, I suppose giving him the fifty *would* be cheaper.'"

"When did *she* get here?" Kevin asked Cathy in a whisper through his teeth. Only outside this family was he more miserable than he was within it.

"Kevin, listen," Cathy said.

"When did she *get* here?" He always hastened to be dislikable, knowing full well that he wasn't going to be liked anyway.

"This afternoon."

"She bring the baby?"

"Yes, and she's—" But the expression on his face, as though the whole family were on a sinking ship and there weren't enough life-belts to go around, made her hesitate. She saw her own reaction to Oona's return, the smallness of it magnified a hundred times, in the way he was acting, and she suddenly realized that she and everyone else in the family needed Kevin. By being what he was he made it possible for everyone else to be, or at least to want to be, what he wasn't. He was what they gave up for Lent—the fattening sweets and starches and the lies and meannesses and ungenerous reactions. So he did have a function in the family, one that made her, for the first time in her life, feel sorry for him.

"She's what?" Kevin was saying. "*What* is she?"

"Sick, Kevin. Wait'll you see her. So go easy. Don't say anything. Go in and be nice. Please!"

He knew she was trying to help him, but could he step out of character now? No one would know him. It would take so much work to *become* known again. And besides, after all these years, hadn't his behavior *become* his attitude? Not toward his mother, whom he loved and treasured. Not even toward his father, who was a nuisance at the business but who at home became a kind of lamplighter of family affection. But toward all the others—toward Oona especially.

"Get away!" he said as Cathy, in a truly amazing attempt to placate him, put her hand on his. It was as if one of his daughters, whom he loved, had turned *into* Cathy, whom he didn't love. "Don't worry, though. I'm not going in. I came by with some money for Papa, so come to the kitchen a minute and I'll give it to you and get *out* of here."

In the kitchen he got out his wallet and began counting out the twenties, tens, and fives that he'd drawn from the Central Hanover Bank that afternoon. He was angry, and yet just handling the bills, the way he could make each one snap and crackle, had the same kind of relaxing effect on him that handling a ball has on an athlete. The crisp, almost inexhaustible existence of money at the Central Hanover Bank fascinated Kevin, and the more he thought about it, about the different denominations in their coffin-like partitions in the teller's drawer, the more he allowed fantasies of wealth and social position to creep like plants into the crevices of his mind. Down at work every morning, while the waiters set the tables and the meat was cut and trimmed, he would sit behind the bar with a pile of magazines on his lap and look at the Bachrach photographs of important men, at the richly colored pictures of statuesque women leaning against cream-colored Lincoln convertibles, and at the ads in which the male-model men of vision, tall and top-heavy like so many of his Wall Street customers, sipped the labeled whiskey that might itself, for all he knew, have been the secret of their success. He would believe for a moment that he too was a success, that he was out in the world making a firm place for himself and his family, putting on a little weight, perhaps, but only insofar as it was justified by a proportionate opulence. But the more he dreamed, the harder, in the end, the transience of the business became, and the more he wanted it to be permanent. The father and husband in him, the warmhearted slob that his wife and daughters knew, that only they were *allowed* to know, had grown prematurely old, and, like all things premature, there was something pathetic and grotesque in his merely being himself.

Just as he was handing Cathy the money (and he even had a rubber band to put around it), they heard their mother calling from the living room.

"Cathy, who is it? Cathy?" Like most people who are hard of hearing, Maggie did not like waiting for an answer. There was always the chance that she had been answered—in a voice too low for her to hear. "Cathy! I said who *is* it?"

Kevin took the money, put it in his pocket, and started in. He had prepared himself, however hastily, to see his parents, Oona, and the baby. So when he entered and saw Jim and Nancy, Oona's allies, as well, he felt trapped and just stood there, a professor of the fact that he was hated. He didn't know what to say and yet could not bear being in the room with them while nothing was being said. Good friends like Jim, Nancy, and Oona dominated their surroundings so, without trying to, without even wanting to. It was too much of a good thing; it was unfair

to the friendless and the unfriendly. Worse by far
was the way Oona's eyes, beneath their long, Arab-
like lashes, seemed to be reflecting his presence with
the lack of involvement almost of inanimate ob-
jects. They were not reacting to his presence,
merely throwing it back.

If only Pa would say something, Oona was thinking, something Kevin or I could use—anything to
break the ice. She looked down out of the corner of
her eye and saw the nervous expansion and con-
traction of leather around the instep of her father's
right shoe, as though his heart were down there, and
while looking she overheard voices in her mind
saying nice things about him. She was tempted to
get into the conversation herself. It's my father
you're talking about. Do you know that?

Even Jim, who used an irreducible minimum of
words in Kevin's presence and who therefore *expected* awkwardness with Kevin around, was becoming intensely conscious of the passing of every
second. He wanted Kevin to say something, even if
it was about the eternal bar and grill and not about
Oona and her baby at all. He wanted to hear
Kevin's voice and detect something in it (he didn't
know what), the way he always detected something,
without knowing what it was, in the voices that
passed his darkened window late at night. But
Kevin couldn't or wouldn't say anything, and
though Jim didn't hold that against him—on the

contrary, he held it in his favor—he could feel something emanating out of the very wordlessness in the room, a miasma of pessimism, the suggestion that in family relations there was always danger. A strong, powerful man with a great capacity for both self-control and violence (once the self-control broke down), he increased the yield of a tense situation by unconsciously lavishing himself upon it. He should not have come back with Oona; he had not wanted to come.

Do you think it's easy being this disliked? Kevin wanted to shout. Try it sometime, you *post*-depression children!

Then he did say something, something so innocuous and ordinary, and yet so evasive of Oona and the baby's presence in the room that it amazed everybody. He had seen how terrible Oona looked and had even *wanted* to greet her in some way. But Jim and Nancy were there, their friendship with Oona was there, the very friendship he was always on the *outside* of, looking in *at*.

So what he said was, simply, "Pa, can I see you for a minute?"

"Aren't you even going to say hello to your sister?" Maggie said. "That's *Oona* sitting there. She just got back from Europe. With a baby!"

"Ma, you stay out of this," Kevin said.

"What kind of a family *is* this?" Maggie went on.

"What's Nancy going to think? Now Kevin, say it, say hello."

"Hello," Kevin said to Oona. He had created this opportunity to be frustrated, made a fool of. Things were going his way.

"Hello," Oona said.

The O'Hagen children gave their mother no more "thought" than they did the trees in the neighborhood or the way Morningside Drive curved down into Amsterdam Avenue at 122nd Street. Nevertheless their mother was as essential to them as a place is where time is ignored as it is lived.

"Now go over and look at the baby," she said.

Kevin turned to her. "You mind your business, Ma." And yet who but his mother in the family treated him as a human being? Who but his mother and wife and children even knew that he *liked* children?

"Go on. See what a big baby she's got. Sheila Penhaligan. Go ahead."

There was nothing to do but go over, and as he did so, Maggie motioned to Oona to get up and go over too. Oona turned to her father, who was too busy seeing that nothing went wrong to have anything to say. Don't you come into this, she said, or tried to say, with that fantastically expressive face of hers. Just sit there. I'm saving you till last in case this other thing, this crazy idea of Mama's that Kevin and I are friends, doesn't work.

She went over and stood by Kevin and the baby. But all Kevin was doing was nodding, and who needed all those nods? Suppose *she* started nodding? She could just hear her mother later: Why did you have to nod too, Oona? Why didn't you help Kevin to *stop* nodding?

So instead of nodding she said, "On the ship on the way over, everybody said the baby was a perfect cross between me and Churchill."

"*Winston* Churchill?" Kevin said, and thought, What makes her *say* these things? For her tone betrayed neither contempt nor amusement. It was another annoyance, this secret life of hers in the remarks she made, in the seemingly harmless way she made them. She belonged elsewhere, with the frivolous, or with people like Jim and Nancy, who did not find her such an object for study. And yet, now that she'd brought Churchill in, he could see what everybody meant. There *was* some Winston Churchill there, around the chubby jawline and cheeks, there really was.

John and Maggie O'Hagen looked on apprehensively, as if from behind the wings. Oona *sounded* sincere. The question was, *was* she?

"Yes, Winston," Oona said. For she could never count on her dislike for a person once the person did or said anything in the least likable. "But then, as I told them, don't *all* babies look a little like Winston Churchill?"

"*All* babies?" Kevin said. He didn't know why, but now that he was talking directly to Oona, and despite the excellent chance of the conversation's becoming a farce if it went on this way much longer, he felt this ridiculous and annoying need to be timid, to keep out of the way of her eyes, which seemed to remain unchanged whether he was looking at them or not. The placidity in them was all wrong; it made her different, a stranger whose personality he was being forced to recognize and accept all at once, instead of gradually over the course of years. He had known about the baby, but now, as Oona and he stood facing each other, each waiting rather awkwardly for the other to say something more, it occurred to him that knowing about the baby was not at all like coming face to face like this with the accomplished fact. It was as if Oona had gone ahead and become herself despite him and his efforts to change or curtail her. All these years, behind his back, she had been slipping out of the pigeonhole he'd put her in, and now here she was, out of it, with a baby, a real baby that she seemed actually to love. At the same time, she more than escaped self-consciousness; her movements seemed to arrive at perfect conclusions unhampered by the slightest awareness on her part. He felt strangely called upon to follow her movements so she would be there at the end of them, and he hated that— hated the way she even made him help her get where she was going.

"You wanted to see me, Kevin?" John O'Hagen said in an effort to rescue Kevin and give him an opportunity to leave. Any conversation between Kevin and Oona was dangerous, but one about Winston Churchill and babies could only lead to disaster.

"Yes, Pa, I did," Kevin said, and followed his father through the apartment to the "maid's" room off the kitchen where his father slept. Kevin had already counted the money, but no sooner did he enter his father's tight tobacco pouch of a room than he removed the rubber band and began counting it again—snap-crackle, crackle-snap—this time on his father's bed.

"I thought I told you on the phone that I'd pick it up on Monday," John O'Hagen said.

"I know. I know you did. I was just passing."

"If you had done as I'd asked—"

"I wouldn't be here now. This wouldn't have happened. Is that it, Pa?" Snap-crackle, crackle-snap: the very feel of the money gave him confidence, angry confidence. "I thought you said she was married."

"She was. The man died. I told you that."

"The man died? Peter Penhaligan died? Did you go to his funeral? Did you see him dead?" This sense of well-being at his father's expense was the closest he came now to loving his father.

"Kevin . . ."

"I'm asking you, Pa. Did you attend the marriage or the funeral?"

"No. I told you, the marriage took place in Maryland."

"And the funeral? Where did that take place?"

"New York. But what's the difference where it took place if the man's dead?"

"He's dead, all right. He was embalmed and laid out at Cooke's on 85th Street and Third Avenue on February tenth of this year."

"How do you know? What did you do, investigate?" Kevin made it so easy for his father to think ill of him (the gratuitous use of the word "embalmed," for example) that his father constantly found himself giving Kevin the benefit of any doubt in an effort to think otherwise. He can't be that much of a bastard, O'Hagen kept telling himself; no one could be.

"If you want to call a few telephone inquiries an investigation, go ahead. I found out, that's all I know."

The conversation stopped here for a moment while Kevin, picking up the count exactly where he had left off, went back to counting again. Snap-crackle, crackle-snap. It was as if he were Aladdin and the money were his lamp. Every so often it must be rubbed, touched, gone back to, for strength, luck, courage. "And he wasn't married. The man they embalmed, Peter Penhaligan, wasn't married."

He was lying, but being alone with his father, in his father's tiny room, the two businessmen of the family, made him realize what a fool Oona had just made of him in the living room with that stupid Winston Churchill stuff. All right, if she could lie about everybody on the ship telling her that the baby looked like Winston Churchill, he could lie about the actual telephone conversation he had had. He had called over a dozen funeral parlors to find out about "a friend of his named Peter Penhaligan," and though a man by that name had been laid out at Cooke's, though he had died of a disease called lupus erythematosus, there had been nothing in their records to indicate that he had been married. Then the man on the phone, because Kevin had said that his friend was married, had said, "Of course, if your friend was secretly married, or married in another country, our records would not necessarily indicate the fact. However, since lupus erythematosus is such an unusual disease, sir, I would advise you to check further."

So Kevin never did find out for certain. Oona had said she was "secretly" married (everything she did was either a secret, a mystery, or a joke), and the man at Cooke's had only added to the possibility that she was telling the truth.

"No married man named Peter Penhaligan was buried in New York this year, Pa," he said.

"But Oona said she was secretly married. When he died it might not have been recorded."

"You believe everything she says, don't you, Pa? Well, I'm telling you, that's an illegitimate child you've got in there." He said it almost exactly as one might have said, There's gold in them thar hills! His most evil moments made you realize how desperately ineffectual he was. You watched him play the devil and knew that this too would end in failure.

"Listen, Kevin. You can stop investigating, because whether the child is illegitimate or not, it's Oona's child and it's staying here. I don't want any more talk like this. To anybody. The child is my grandchild. Remember that."

If Kevin had left the apartment then, nothing would have happened. But laughter—the suggestion of friendliness and warmth—was coming from the living room, and he was drawn to it as a hungry man is to food. If they weren't going to give him some, he was going to sprinkle it with arsenic.

"Will you have a drink?" O'Hagen said in an effort to learn Kevin's intentions.

"No. I'm leaving." He slipped on his topcoat and started in to say goodbye.

"You don't have to go in, Kevin," O'Hagen said. "I mean if you don't want to. I'll say you were in a hurry."

"I know I don't have to, Pa." There was more laughter. Oona was saying something; it was turning into a regular party. "I thought you'd want me to. I know Ma would."

Even then, if he hadn't decided on the way in to slip his gloves on, nothing would have happened. But it was the old familiar performance all over again, only this time in reverse. Watch carefully, ladies and gentlemen, and you will see my fingers disappear one at a time. Everybody watched the performance for a moment, and it was actually in an attempt to include him in the fun that Oona said, "Nothing gives one the courage to be oneself like self-expression in some art form."

"What does that mean?" Kevin said. He knew he was making himself comprehensible to her by blushing, but that only made him blush more. As a child she had been a prolific creator of emotion in others, a beautiful blond green-eyed thing full of surprises either improvised on the spot or sprung with precision (usually at the dinner table) in the form of chance remarks. Even during the overcrowded years on Amsterdam Avenue, when everyone was self-absorbed if only not to go mad, she had provided herself with most of the family's attention.

"It doesn't mean anything. I was joking. I'm sorry," Oona said.

But her apology, touching as it did upon a whole reservoir of family feelings—feelings he didn't trust, couldn't feel, and never would express—only made it worse.

"You all hate me, don't you? Hate me. You think I don't know that? You think I care? Tell me something, though, you funny people. Mama and Papa die, who's going to bury them, pay the funeral expenses? You funny people going to pay?"

Jim suddenly realized that he had already lost the capacity to be bereaved by Kevin's death. For years, just by staying alive, Kevin had robbed him even of that. My brother, he thought, for the loss was even greater now by being no loss at all.

"Why don't you thank Kevin now," Oona said to her mother and father, "while you're still alive?"

Kevin appeared on the verge of becoming someone else with rage. He looked at her, his lips stretched like rubber bands over his bared teeth, the knuckles of his clenched fingers white, his arms straight down and quivering like hot pokers in his torso. "Shut up, you . . . you . . . slut!"

Jim sprang from his chair. "Who are you calling a slut? You swine!" The tears coming from his eyes would have made him look pathetic if the whole lower part of his face hadn't been almost vicious. The tears were something he couldn't help; they had nothing to do with him; he might have been angry in the rain.

"Stop it! Stop it, do you hear?" Maggie said.

But Jim stepped up to him, his face vicious and full of hate, his head thrust forward like a bull's, the muscles and cartilage in his thick neck bulging. "I remember as a kid, when I used to stutter, how you used to make fun of me, how you imitated me, even when I had something to say that I thought was important, something I really wanted to say. I remember when I started to go out with girls and you were working and making money and buying clothes, how you made me beg you for hours for permission to use one of your neckties or shirts, a lousy pair of shoes. And I remember you nagging Mama about Oona, your long faces when Mama, thank God, allowed Oona to go on being crazy— what you called worthless! You, you're the worthless one. You're worse than that. You're all the things that people cut and squeeze out of themselves, patched up to look like a man. You don't even belong here. You're a mistake!"

Kevin knew, though he was as big and strong as Jim, that a fight between them could end in only one way—the death of one or the other. No matter how long the fight lasted or how bloody it became or how many times Jim might seem to be defeated, he knew that Jim would allow it to end only when death ended it. And Kevin did not want to die, let alone be arrested for killing.

But suddenly, in that split second when Maggie's scream ("Stop it! God, stop!") seemed to express what was possible rather than forbid it from happening, Jim was struck—struck so solidly on the jaw that he fell, was sent flying backward against the piano.

"Forgive me, Jim. I'm sorry." It was his father. "But I couldn't have you saying those things."

"All right, Pa. Forget it," Jim said, and thought, Blessed are the Kevins of this world, for they shall receive compassion and whatever extra money is lying around.

"Do you forgive me, Jim?"

Jim looked up at the burned, florid face above him, and for a moment it was as if his father were the Bowery bum he and Nancy had encountered down at Irving Place. Could his childhood fear at the sight of the bums on that old Morningside Park bench have had some basis in reality? Was there something between his father and Kevin that made his father a bum?

"Yes, Pa"—it was like giving the Irving Place derelict a quarter—"I forgive you," he said. But he was conscious of an instinctive repulsion, a feeling of disgust for this man who did not know when to stop protecting Kevin, who was more interested in being understood himself, in forgiving and being forgiven, than in being fair. He even hated himself for forgiving his father—hated all people who forgave easily because they not only wanted to be as easily forgiven, they never hesitated to do unforgivable things. It was this cheapening of forgiveness, this moral sentimentality, that had made his father, and even at times Oona, his models of how not to be. Jim's outstanding quality was unfortunately— perhaps inevitably, considering his old stuttering stigma—tied to his great fault. He was profoundly loyal on the one hand and deeply unforgiving on the other. Indeed, the one thing he would not or could not forgive was a breach of loyalty itself, which meant that while acquaintances to whom he owed nothing were forgiven almost everything, friends to whom he owed a great deal were forgiven almost nothing.

John O'Hagen took Jim's arm to help him up and was thankful, deeply thankful, that Jim didn't pull away. But would he ever, no matter how much longer he lived, be able to explain to Jim that he had struck him not because the vicious words were lies but because they weren't? Would Jim ever understand that he could not allow everybody's hatred of Kevin to be brought this way into the open? Or was he deceiving himself? Was he protecting Kevin and the family, or the "emergency" fund that he wanted at all costs to be kept secret? Like most men who turn inward late in life, O'Hagen had an innocent man's attitude toward himself, and with it an unwitting tendency to expose to himself his own guilt.

Everybody was silent now with Jim back on his feet, and as Oona watched them, the three men, it was as if the family's years of life were sliding or passing one within another, backward and forward, until what was happening in the room became confused with what had happened in the room or might happen again. The three of them, the men, were as they had always been; they were themselves, only more so. They were like very old newspapers, the kind she had once leafed through (for an extension course at Columbia) down in the newspaper stacks of Butler Library. The newspapers were twenty, thirty, even forty years old, and what struck her most was not the marvelously lean advertisements of cloche hats and fringe dresses, but the deadness, the retrospective ineffectuality, of so much of the opinion and self-righteous indignation in the newsprint itself. In one old New York *Evening World*, for example, there was a picture of Teddy Roosevelt with a caption reading, "I am as strong as a bull moose." His face was fierce and menacing, his right arm reminiscent of the label on the Arm and Hammer washing soda box. It was obvious that when the picture was taken Teddy Roosevelt did not believe in death, let alone in his own, and Oona, seeing his fantastic vitality and confidence through the knowledge that he was long since dead, learned what perhaps only women are capable of learning. How could he not have known it wasn't that important to be as strong as a bull moose? She had thought in the privacy of her cubicle, with her own face in darkness and the spotlight on his. Did he know now—now that he was dead?

Suddenly she turned to the three of them, her

father, Kevin, and Jim, and cried, "You fools! Don't you know that in ten, twenty, thirty or forty years from now, we'll all be gone? Why can't we get along now? I come home with a baby and this has to happen. Why? What's the matter with everybody?" She hesitated, ran a hand across her forehead and eyes. The amazement, Maderini had said, if only we didn't lose that. Is this what he had meant? "As soon as I find a place," she said, "I'll live somewhere else." She was sick; she felt sick. They had all been telling her the truth.

"You're living here," O'Hagen said. "You're staying here." He turned to Kevin, who was compulsively putting the finishing touches to his gloves. New pair; the fingers had to be broken in, God damn it! "I'll see you on Monday, Kevin."

As Kevin turned to leave, Jim started toward the bathroom to run a cold washrag over his face. He felt no love, no regret, no charity. He felt nothing, and Kevin was his brother, the brother whose reputation in the neighborhood he had so often, and so blindly, defended with his fists.

"Is that all?" Maggie said. "My two sons . . ." There were tears rolling down her cheeks; she couldn't go on. Her whole life, it seemed, had been a failure.

"Yes, Ma," Jim said. "That's all."

The men, each one as strong as a bull moose, had spoken.

CHAPTER XVII

"Oona, did you get a call from a man at the Italian Consulate today?" Jim said.

"Yes. He said you gave him Mama's number."

They were at the hospital, sitting on a bench outside the staff's private offices. Oona had finally agreed to an examination and they were waiting for the specialist with whom Jim had arranged an appointment.

"This letter was in our box for you," Jim said. "From Italy."

Oona turned it back side up, positive it was from Dr. Maderini. It wasn't. Friedensohn, the return address said, Dr. Anthony Friedensohn. She slit it open with her nail and read:

Dear Oona,

I deserted you in Italy. You think that, and you have a right to. I beg you however to believe that if the baby had not been born prematurely, I would have tried once more to persuade you to go to a hospital. In fact when you refused the first time, and I assumed it was because you were against going

to a hospital in Florence, I made arrangements for
you at a hospital in Genoa. I made them without
my wife's knowledge several days before the baby
was born, Oona. You must believe that.

After the birth, when I found out what you had
gone through, I felt that I had lost whatever right I
might still have had to see you. Dr. Maderini was
taking care of you.

As for money, I did not want to resort to that
kind of "proof" that I still felt responsible. I *am*
weak, Oona. I always told you that, and you, God
bless you, always contradicted me with such vehemence that there were times when I almost
believed in myself as much as you wanted to believe
in me.

I am however responsible for my daughter, and so
I have set up what is known as an irrevocable
trust—for you and for her—in America. A lawyer
from the Italian Consulate will be getting in touch
with you about it, if he hasn't already. More will be
added to it as time goes on, and there will of course
be interest accumulations, but at the moment it
amounts to $20,000. Not much, but it will grow, I
promise you, and on her seventeenth birthday, with
college just ahead, you as her mother and guardian
will receive the first check. From her twenty-first
birthday on, the checks will automatically be made
out in her name. At the present time, however, you
will receive $300 a month for her support. The

lawyer will explain it all so I won't bother.

Time has passed, Oona, so please don't let your Irish pride come to the fore now. Nothing can be done about the trust anyway. The money in question can accrue only to the girl, our daughter, not to you, not to me. When I say "our" daughter, please don't misunderstand me. I will never attempt to see her, and never attempt to tell her who her father is.

In closing, allow me to say once more that I did make arrangements in Genoa for you before the baby was born. I would like you to believe that, and if you do, and you would tell me in a note that you do, I would treasure the note as I still do my memory of you.

Goodbye Oona
TONY FRIEDENSOHN

"Oona, what is it?" Jim said. For it was as if her face had suddenly been seized by her own unorthodoxy. She has just been laughing with him, fooling around, and now . . . "You're crying," he said.

"I am?" She knew she was, but she had said to herself, Don't try to find out why. To hell with it. She hadn't cried about Tony for a long time, and it gave her a nice feeling about him—about herself. Like those late afternoons at the Institute of Ophthalmology, waiting for him in the clinic, watching him go about his business. Those were the times, with his eyes and mind elsewhere, when she had felt most alive to him, loved him almost without knowing it—when there had been no desire to outknow what she was doing by finding out why she was doing it.

She handed Jim the letter, and as he read it she regained control of herself. "Remember in one of my letters, Jim, when I said that about Jewish fathers being slobs?"

"Yes, and you meant it as a compliment."

"Maybe I did. One cheer instead of three."

He handed the letter back. "He sounds all right, Oona, like a real human being. I'm happy for you."

"I'll be able to pay my way at Mama's now. And breathe a little."

"And buy some clothes," Jim added, "and go out with men."

"You think I should?" Other men were in her voice, even as she said it—an irrepressible honey, the food of love.

"You're going to, whether you should or not. But of course you should. You should also get married." He looked up; a nurse was motioning to him. "Come on. Dr. Stimson's ready for you. Now, don't be nervous. I'll speak to him afterward and see you right here before you leave. All right?"

The examination took over an hour and when Jim spoke to Dr. Stimson, a tall elderly man with white hair, the specialist said, "That man in Italy, Dr. Maderini, was right, Jim. Nephritis."

"What do you think, Doctor?"

"Do you know what that girl could use? A little luck. That doesn't sound very medical, does it? But I mean, right now, good things should happen to her. She's that kind of girl—full of fun. Likes to laugh and kid around. She wasn't in here ten minutes before we were both laughing. Sadness is what that girl doesn't need. And some people do, you know. Some people thrive on sadness."

"You're right about Oona, Doctor, and speaking of good luck, she just got some. A trust fund has been set up for her and her daughter."

"That's exactly what I mean. She shouldn't have to worry. The disease will run its course, but with luck it will take a long time. Keep an eye on her, Jim. Look after her. See that she doesn't ever become run down."

"Don't worry, Doctor. I will. And thank you. Thank you very much."

They shook hands and Jim rejoined Oona in the hallway.

"Well," Oona said. "What did he say?"

"He likes you, Oona. He really does."

"What was it, an audition?"

"No, I mean he said, well, what I've been telling

you. What I'm going to go right on telling you. Do you hear?"

"All right, Jim. Kiss me once, because I feel happy and you're so—I was going to say sweet, but I don't know what you are. What are you?"

"Sweet." He kissed her.

"I've got an appointment with that man from the Italian Consulate, Jim. I'll see you and Nancy tonight maybe. All right?" Her expectations never went beyond the immediate future, which was perhaps why she was so demanding of the present. The forestalling of a pleasure, even when it meant possibly increasing it, was beyond her power.

"Fine," Jim said. "Nancy and I will be home all evening."

Watching her go was a little like losing the conviction that he had just been enjoying her company. And so, as usual, he watched harder as those crazy thin legs of hers took her farther and farther away from him down the hall. Good luck, Oona, he thought as she passed through the revolving door. Good luck.

Printed in the United States
872800001B